CAMINO REAL*

* USE ANGLICIZED PRONUNCIATION:

Cá-mino *Ré*-al (TW)

BY TENNESSEE WILLIAMS

PLAYS

Baby Doll & Tiger Tail

Camino Real (with Ten Blocks on the Camino Real)

Candles to the Sun

Cat on a Hot Tin Roof

Clothes for a Summer Hotel

Fugitive Kind

A House Not Meant to Stand

The Glass Menagerie

A Lovely Sunday for Creve Coeur

Mister Paradise and Other One-Act Plays:
These Are the Stairs You Got to Watch, Mister Paradise, The Palooka, Escape, Why Do You Smoke So Much, Lily?, Summer At The Lake, The Big Game, The Pink Bedroom, The Fat Man's Wife, Thank You Kind Spirit, The Municipal Abattoir, Adam and Eve on a Ferry, And Tell Sad Stories of The Deaths of Queens...

Not About Nightingales

The Notebook of Trigorin

Something Cloudy, Something Clear

Spring Storm

Stairs to the Roof

Stopped Rocking and Other Screen Plays:
All Gaul is Divided, The Loss of a Teardrop Diamond, One Arm, Stopped Rocking

A Streetcar Named Desire

Sweet Bird of Youth (with The Enemy: Time)

The Traveling Companion and Other Plays:
The Chalky White Substance, The Day on Which a Man Dies, A Cavalier for Milady, The Pronoun 'I', The Remarkable Rooming-House of Mme. Le Monde, Kirche Küche Kinder, Green Eyes, The Parade, The One Exception, Sunburst, Will Mr. Merriwether Return from Memphis?, The Traveling Companion

27 Wagons Full of Cotton and Other Plays:
27 Wagons Full of Cotton, The Purification, The Lady of Larkspur Lotion, The Last of My Solid Gold Watches, Portrait of a Madonna, Auto-Da-Fé, Lord Byron's Love Letter, The Strangest Kind of Romance, The Long Goodbye, Hello From Bertha, This Property is Condemned, Talk to Me Like the Rain and Let Me Listen, Something Unspoken

The Two-Character Play

Vieux Carré

Jo Van Fleet as Marguerite Gautier and Hurd Hatfield as
Lord Byron in a publicity still by Edwin Erbe for the
original Broadway production of *Camino Real*.

CAMINO REAL

BY TENNESSEE WILLIAMS

INTRODUCTION BY JOHN GUARE

A NEW DIRECTIONS BOOK

CONTENTS

AN INTRODUCTION IN
NINETEEN BLOCKS

BLOCK ONE
NEW HAVEN BRANCH

In the fall of 1960, the Yale School of Drama accepted me as a playwright. My true life was beginning. Finally to be out of dread, claustrophobic college, class of 1960, and into the real world of the theater—class of forever!

The dean of the Drama School welcomed us. "Get lost," he told us. A murmur went up in the audience. Did he just say *get lost*? The dean slowly turned the page of his speech, "—in the world of the theater."

Yes! That's what I'm here to do. Get lost! Hadn't Leslie Fiedler written in a 1958 essay called "The Un-Angry Young Men" that American culture had "never been in a duller or less promising condition" than now. But the new now was 1960 and you could feel urgency happening. In that year alone I had already seen Godard's *Breathless*, Truffaut's *The Four Hundred Blows*, Beckett's *Krapp's Last Tape* and Albee's *The Zoo Story*. I'm arriving at the dawn of a new sensibility, a *nouvelle vague*. Surf's up! I'm in!

The first production that year on the main stage would be the Scottish play. Isn't *Macbeth* bad luck? But isn't it all about ambition. We were all ambition personified. The first question among my fellow Yale playwrights was scoping out which of us would be the first to hit Broadway!

I sneaked into the balcony of the university theater to watch the closed rehearsals of the Scottish play. The director stopped the actors midscene: "No no, Judy, listen to how it should be done." The actors gathered at the edge of the stage. The director reverently dropped a needle onto a long-playing record that sat on a phonograph at the foot of the stage and listened to the English actors Maurice Evans and Dame Judith Anderson intone the roles of Lord and Lady Macbeth in a recording of a recent television production. The Yale actors then imitated the record.

Please don't say this is the way it's going to be.

The Shubert Theater was another point of excitement about being in New Haven. In those days, new Broadway plays would play out of town to purify themselves before coming into the holy grail of Broadway. One of the first plays to open that fall of 1960 would be the world premiere of the new Tennessee Williams' play *Period of Adjustment*.

Elia Kazan's 1959 production of Tennessee's *Sweet Bird of Youth* had overwhelmed me in spite of some nasty reviews. It was the first time I'd seen mixed media onstage—film used to heighten the political rally at the end of act two; plus Paul Newman got castrated at the end. I'd be seeing Tennessee's latest while the blood was still wet on it.

What a depressing event: *Period of Adjustment* was an adorable romantic comedy with a heavy symbol—a house perched on top of a fault—a crack in the earth—domestic squabbles—but everybody ended up happily. No, this can't be Tennessee. I had done my undergraduate thesis on tearful comedy, sentimental comedy—*comedie larmoyante*—comedy with the teeth removed. This kind of Broadway comedy was the death of comedy. Had Tennessee gone over to the other side?

The Yale writing classes stressed Ibsen Ibsen Ibsen. The well-crafted play. Even Chekhov wasn't safe. Chekhov structured in molasses, Ibsen structured in steel! You craft a play—w.r.i.g.h.t. A wheelwright fashions a wheel, a wainwright a wain (whatever a wain was), a playwright fashions his plays and Ibsen is the model. You think Albee avant garde? No no *The Zoo Story* is pure Ibsen. Really? Where? Hadn't Godard recently said "a story should have a beginning, a middle and an end, but not necessarily in that order." Where's the Ibsen in that? What about Ionesco? What about *Godot*? Brecht? Nary a mention. Serious plays meant not a laugh; comedies meant no meat.

What was I doing in this Ivy League world of secret societies? People there had an ease that eluded me. Had life withheld a secret so freely given to everyone else in New Haven. Why hadn't I run off to sea or to South America? I could tell you why: had I not been in school, I'd have been drafted into the army pronto. Yale supplied me with a student deferment. I wanted real life but on my terms. Also the brand name of Yale allowed my parents who were supporting me to say Johnny's at Yale. Also I was afraid but that was a secret. I'd endure a year. But at what price?

A few weeks after the Scottish play finished its deadly run, the Dramat, the Yale undergrad drama organization, took over the University theater stage to put on Tennessee Williams' *Camino Real*.

Why bother? *Camino Real* was a famous dud seven years before in 1953, right? I had never bothered to read it. Hadn't Walter Kerr called it "the worst play by the best playwright of his generation"? I had ignored the existence of *Camino Real* as you would an embarrassing relative. Elia Kazan, who had directed the perfection of *A Streetcar Named Desire*, had staged *Camino*. If Kazan and Tennessee together couldn't make it work, how good can it be? I loved Tennessee—at least pre-*Period of Adjustment* which had moved on to Broadway to die. And now this turkey was being performed—by undergraduates! I might as well add one more entry to my list of reasons for standing on the New Haven money-back line.

BLOCK TWO
Two Ways to Pronounce It

A town square. A fancy hotel on one side—a flop house on the other—in the center a gateway to a desert. *Terra incognita*. Spanish music played. Don Quixote came down the center aisle of the theater onto the stage asking where he was. Sancho Panza read their location from a map:

> ". . .the square of a walled town which is the end of the Camino Real
> and the beginning of the Camino Real. Halt there . . . and turn back,
> Traveler, for the spring of humanity has gone dry in this place . . ."

Wait! The town has two names? One pronunciation meant the grand ancient way—the other pronounced real is grim reality. I was in my own *Camino Real*—the grand way caMEEEno reAL was the Yale of my dreams—the CAmino Reel was the Yale I was living in, the life "where the spring of humanity has gone dry."

I still remember the moment when an airplane, *il fugitivo*, landed in this strange town to rescue a few lucky refugees and deliver them to freedom. Powerful red lights blasted from the back of the house. Refugees ran up the aisle to get on board. Iron gates dropped down barring the rest of the people onstage from getting on. The sound of the plane's taking off became deafening. The lights moved upwards. The plane flew away. The cast onstage and we in the audience looked up as our last chance at freedom flew away. Confetti dropped down on us, falling in our mouths. We were left behind. Would I ever have the luck to find my *il fugitivo* that would transport me to my true life? The gypsy in the play said it best: "Baby, your luck ran out the day you were born."

How did this play know me so well?

It also advised me: "Make voyages! Attempt them! There's nothing else!"

Where had this play been? Everybody argued about it. What's it about? Is it political? Is it existential? If it's an allegory, it's an allegory of what? I could answer that. It was the allegory of me!

It was the allegory of my existence in 1960. That terror on that stage was my terror. Its fear of the *terra incognita* beyond the city walls—its understanding of how it feels not to be understood and be trapped and yearn for escape on *il fugitivo*, any transport that might take me to freedom which might perhaps be only another ring of hell. Kilroy lost his golden gloves. Kilroy had his heart "as big as the head of a baby" cut out of him. Brecht said we weren't supposed to identify with a play's characters— *Verfremdungseffekt!*—but this was different. I *was* Kilroy. How can this Kilroy not end up with the other corpses in the *Camino Real* street cleaner's barrels? Get lost? How could I be anything but?

Camino needed to tell its truth so urgently that it had to break the fourth wall between the stage and us out there in the audience. It spoke with a rage and a joy. It was so funny. The live music wouldn't let you sit still. This play didn't give me any answers but it sure spoke to the problems.

Camino Real also must have given voice to the terror of the Dramat undergraduates who had surrendered to the spirit of Tennessee's play. They were all about to graduate out of the safety of school and plunge into the real world—the question of the moment for everyone was the eternal: how will I live my life? Who'll speak for me?

The gypsy's daughter offered a prayer:

"God bless all con men and hustlers and pitchmen who hawk their hearts on the street, all two-time losers who're likely to lose once more, the courtesan who made the mistake of love, the greatest of lovers crowned with the longest of horns, the poet who wandered far from his heart's green country and possibly will and possibly won't be able to find his way back, look down with a smile tonight on the last cavaliers, the ones with rusty armor and soiled white plumes, and visit with understanding and something that's almost tender those fading legends that come and go in this plaza like songs not clearly remembered, oh, sometime and somewhere, let there be something to mean the word honor again! . . . *And, oh, God, let me dream tonight of the Chosen Hero!*"

I wanted a chosen hero. I also wanted to *be* the hero of choice. She was praying for us in the audience. Those self-pitying freaks and outlaws and losers and noble dreamers on that stage were my people—people without a plan, living day to day by the seat of their pants. People like me without a clue. This was a bracing theater where the sky wasn't a bright canary yellow, where life wasn't a bowl of cherries. I got rhythm? Forget it. You'll never walk alone? Baby, there's no other way to walk. Why did *Camino Real* feel subversive? Could it be it was telling us the truth?

Antonin Artaud had written in *No More Masterpieces*:

"I therefore propose a theatre in which violent physical images crush and hypnotize the sensibilities of the spectators who are caught in the theatre as if they were in a whirlwind of superior forces."

Artaud's ideal theater would "give us all back the natural and magical equivalent of the dogmas in which we no longer believe." Artaud's sought-for theater would have the power of restoring "the theatre back to its primitive purpose, replacing it in its religious and metaphysical aspect, reconciling it with the universe."

In 1960, I didn't yet know the work of this great visionary but when I finally did read him, I knew I had been there.

I looked at everyone around me in my Connecticut Camino with new eyes. We all had the same secret. We all were scared shitless.

BLOCK THREE
How To Make It Mine

When we loathe a play, a movie, a book, we have so many fecal words at our disposal: a piece of shit—I want it out of me—It made me want to throw up—expulsion! But when we see something we love, words lose their gymnastic dexterity: "I was speechless." For a writer, loving something is no less than the delivery of a question that asks, if you love me this much, how will you incorporate me into you? An imperative that says: "steal from me." Borrow from me. Let me infiltrate into your very bones.

Camino dared me in a way I had never been challenged. In 1956, Tyrone Guthrie's production of Marlowe's *Tamburlaine the Great* played on Broadway for a short run. When Tamburlaine unrolled an enormous map of the world across the entire stage of the Winter Garden theater and strode across it, claiming the world as his own, I knew if I was going to be a playwright, I would have to write that! But how? Marlowe's play was British and written a long time before. How could I dare step on any map and claim anything as my own?

But *Camino Real* was American and written by someone who had just been in New Haven a few weeks before. I had just seen a map of an unknown world strewn in front of me by a poet who was also a playwright. *Camino Real* gave us unarmed people bravado to stumble out into the world. But what world? How would I make *Camino* part of me?

BLOCK FOUR
THE LIVING ROOM

Suddenly Yale was different from anywhere else. Thanks to the spark of inspiration delivered by *Camino*, New Haven suddenly looked like Paris in the '20s. Did I see the irony back then? That this play about existential anguish and isolation was the cattle prod that made me feel I belonged.

I made friends. We talked about the future. I ushered at the plays which opened at the Shubert almost every week, studying the authors as they paced in the back row so I'd know how to behave when my turn came. All the plays seemed to take place in living rooms: *All the Way Home* (based on a James Agee novella which removed Agee's voice, made it a soap opera and won that year's Pulitzer); *Under the Yum-Yum* tree (an aging roué discovers true love in his pursuit of a young virgin); *A Far Country* (a young handsome Freud analyzed a paralyzed Kim Stanley and allowed her to walk at the final curtain). Hey! Where's the poetry? Then who showed up at Yale to speak to us? T.S. Eliot! There he was! Right there onstage at Woolsey Hall! What did he say? I have no idea. His presence put a blizzard of white noise in my head. *Il Fugitivo* had let me escape from my own personal "Waste Land." I wrote and wrote. I had my new play accepted for production in the directors' workshop.

On Broadway that season I saw a few challenging plays. *The Hostage* by Brendan Behan, Shelagh Delaney's *A Taste of Honey*, Ionesco's *Rhinoceros* (starring Eli Wallach—the original Kilroy). But those plays were Irish, English, French. You could ask challenging questions if the play had the snob cache of success on a British stage.

BLOCK FIVE
WHERE DID YOU COME FROM?

Two versions of *Camino Real* existed—the two-act play I'd seen and an earlier one-act version called *Ten Blocks on the Camino Real* that Tennessee had worked on at the same time as he was struggling with *Streetcar*. Both *Caminos* were beauties.

The first mention I could find of it was a poem Tennessee had written in 1945 called "Camino Real." A section in it ended up in the one act version

> . . .lots of babies who've never been properly weaned
> from Hotel Statler room service
> can still make sing, or make like magnificent singing,
> canaries in bed-springs.

Tennessee said in his *Memoirs*:

> ". . .I wrote the first draft of *Camino* in New Orleans in 1946; that was the manuscript Audrey Wood told me to put away and not show to anybody. Her reaction had depressed me so that I thought the play must really be quite awful. Then, a few years later, I was in New York and dropped by the Actor's Studio. Kazan was conducting an exercise with Eli Wallach and Barbara Baxley and some other student actors—and they were performing *10 Blocks on the Camino Real*. I realized that Audrey had been altogether mistaken, that it played remarkably well, and I said, 'Oh, Kazan, we must do this. We must do this with one other play, maybe, for Broadway.' There was no Off-Broadway in those days; he agreed . . . I continued to work on it and expanded it into *Camino Real*."

Elia Kazan, the director of *Streetcar* and Miller's *Death of a Salesman* and one of the founders of the Actors Studio, apparently had been unhappy with his work in 1942 on Thornton Wilder's *The Skin of Our Teeth* and wanted to explore, in the confines of Actor's Studio, the challenges of acting fantasy truthfully and adding a new dimension to the naturalistic American acting style.

In 1952, Kazan asked Marlon Brando to return to the stage in a double bill of two of Tennessee's one acts: *Ten Blocks on the Camino Real* and *27 Wagons Full of Cotton* on Broadway. (Where else? Off-Broadway did not exist.) When Brando did not accept the offer (something about his spiritual advisers as well a new movie), Kazan prompted Tennessee to expand *Ten Blocks* into what would be its catastrophic 1953 Broadway production.

Tennessee's world-wide success with *Streetcar* had not made him any the less *fugitivo*. He returned with a fury into the world he had created. At the beginning of both versions of *Camino*, the fountain in the plaza may be dry but not the fountain gushing out of Tennessee's fervid imagination. Tennessee found firm footing in the world of this play.

Here was a chance for a truly poetic theater to come alive in the mainstream of Broadway, breaking the stranglehold of naturalism on its audiences and create a tradition that would enrich generations of playwrights and actors and directors and designers and audiences for years to come.

Wait! Was it possible that the ten in *Ten Blocks on the* . . . referred to Tennessee himself who signed his letters 10? Was it autobiographical? Is the town square of *Camino Real* merely the naturalistic landscape of success?

"The violets in the mountains have broken the rocks!"

They didn't.

Eli Wallach said in his memoirs that rehearsals were joyous. No one was prepared for the hostile response.

Walter Kerr wrote in an open letter to Tennessee Williams in the *New York Herald Tribune,* April 13, 1953:

> "What terrifies me about *Camino Real* is not what you want to say
> but the direction in which you, as an artist, are moving. You're
> heading toward the cerebral; don't do it."

Kazan blamed *Camino Real*'s failure on the wrong realistic scenic design; it should have had the feel of a painting by a Latino painter named Posada whose work featured skulls and flowers.

Forget it. The audience of Eisenhower's America did not choose to be spoken to by this play: No gypsy's daughter has the right to pray for me. Eric Bentley called it: Camino Unreal. Brooks Atkinson said in *The New York Times* review "Even the people who respect Mr. Williams' courage and recognize his talent are likely to be aghast by what he has to say." Lewis Kronenberger wrote in 1952-1953 edition of the best plays of the year series:

"I had to reject [*Camino Real*]: for by my lights *Camino Real* is a serious failure. It seems to me not just the failure of a method, or even of a vision, but the most self-indulgent misuse of a talent . . . the play emerges a patchwork of every manner from Lorca to *Hellzapoppin'* . . . Elia Kazan staged the play very vividly as theatre; it doubtless defied being anything else . . ."

Kronenberg's ten best plays of 1952-1953 were Arthur Miller's *The Crucible*, Inge's Pulitzer Prize wining *Picnic*, plus Frederick Knott's *Dial M for Murder* (British), Sam and Bella Spewack's *My Three Angels* (adapted from the French), Peter Ustinov's *Love of Four Colonels* (British), and the Leonard Bernstein, Comden and Green musical *Wonderful Town*, *The Time of the Cuckoo* by Arthur Laurents (a spinster finds romance in Venice), *Climate of Eden* by Moss Hart ("the most original drama so far the season and in writing, staging and acting, the most distinguished," John Chapman of the *Daily News*), *Bernadine* by Mary Chase (teenage boys invent an ideal woman who only says "yes"), and *The Emperor's Clothes* by George Tabori (Hungarian police state, circa 1930).

BLOCK SIX
SIDEBAR

I've always had a secret bone to pick with *The Crucible*. Why doesn't John Proctor go mad if everyone else in Salem is driven nuts by the events of the witch hunt? Why does Proctor get spared? Miller had said in the last lines of his adaptation of Ibsen's *Enemy of the People*: "the strong are always lonely." John Proctor always seems too far above the fray, as if he represents the audience who can watch him and say, "Hello. I'm also John Proctor. I'm the mirror of you. I'm strong. I'm lonely. You and me? We'd never fold." What would happen if John Proctor woke up to find he'd made a stop on the *Camino Real*?

BLOCK SEVEN
A Detour to London

Did anyone like *Camino Real*? In 1954, Kenneth Tynan in London responded to its effect. British playwrights "should not ape the Americans, but at least learn from them". Arthur Miller and Tennessee Williams were full of love for "the bruised individual soul," Tynan quoted *Camino Real*:

GUTMAN: They pay the price of admission, the same as you.

LADY MULLIGAN: What price is that?

GUTMAN: Desperation.

Kathleen Tynan wrote in her biography of her husband: "The recipe for drama—self-knowledge through desperation—became the cornerstone of (Tynan's) critical theory."

BLOCK EIGHT
Other Worlds?

Tennessee Williams wrote in *The New York Times* the Sunday before *Camino Real* opened in 1953: "More than any other work that I have done, this play has seemed to me like the construction of another world, a separate existence."

The construction of another world, a separate existence. What did that even mean? How do you create another world without making it sound like ballet—or opera—or fairy tale—or science fiction?

Ever since naturalism became the reigning sensibility of mainstream theater in the nineteenth century, directors and writers sought a poetic equivalent. Gordon Craig in England—Meyerhold in Russia—playwrights like Maeterlinck—challenged the naturalistic constrictions of bourgeois theater. Eugene O'Neill leapt into poetry with *The Emperor Jones*, but fell flat with plays like *The Great God Brown, Lazarus Laughed* and *Days Without End* (but his masterpieces were naturalistic: *Long Day's Journey Into Night, The Iceman Cometh*).

Had poetic theater in America found its home only in musical theater? An audience could accept poetry with a few hit tunes and dances thrown in.

BLOCK NINE
Is Poetry Fancy Talk?

In the 1930s the American playwright Maxwell Anderson wrote highly regarded verse dramas in iambic pentameter about people as diverse as Queen Elizabeth in *Elizabeth the Queen* and Sacco and Vanzetti in *Winterset*:

> In all these turning lights I find no clue,
> only a masterless night, and in my blood
> no certain answer, yet is my mind my own,
> yet is my heart a cry toward something dim
> in distance, which is higher than I am
> and makes me emperor of the endless dark
> even in seeking!

They are unreadable today—and unperformed.

In the early '50s, the arrival on Broadway of successful British poetic plays like T. S. Eliot's *The Cocktail Party* and Christopher Fry's *The Lady's Not For Burning* and *Venus Observed* heralded a new Elizabethan era. Its effect didn't pan out. The poetry in those plays was all in the language: fanciful verse didn't come out of enormous poetic actions but rather felt sprayed onto essentially naturalistic domestic settings.

Tennessee was talking about "another world"—a theater where large events inspired the visual and aural poetry. A theater that was American and was accepted by American audiences.

BLOCK TEN
Who Are Your Parents?

In the late 1930s the playwright William Saroyan had a brief skyrocket of a career, most notably with his anarchic *The Time Of Your Life* (it won a Pulitzer Prize which he rejected). His bold voice pointed a new direction for the American theater.

In 1941, Tennessee read Saroyan's latest play *Jim Dandy* and wrote his agent, Audrey Wood:

"[. . .it's] the maddest thing he has yet written. Still it has an unearthly charm. People go round and round for no reason in [a] revolving door, walk with one foot in imaginary coffins, sit in chair on table, dance, sing, change shoes, play cornet and pianola, recline on a Mae West bed, make rhapsodic speeches about the snow and the rain—all in the room of a San Francisco public library. . . . Undoubtedly a parable on the subject of LIFE—I cannot understand the symbolism, more than barely. But I read it twice and I must admit I was fascinated and moved by the strangeness of it and occasional speeches ring the bell of pure poetry."

Tennessee wrote a fan letter to Saroyan:

"[. . . your play] . . . rings in my head and heart like the multitude of soft and musical bells that bring down the curtain. It is a beautiful little mystery of a play . . . [which] began to glow and vibrate, coming out like a star in 'first dark.' "

Saroyan, who was "fed up with the fat-headedness of Broadway," replied to the unknown Williams: ". . .there is no one in the American theatre who knows how to do anything other than the ordinary, banal, commercial and shabby. . . ."

In 1942 Thornton Wilder's *The Skin of Our Teeth* opened on Broadway to acclaim and popular acceptance and a Pulitzer Prize. Was this the dreamed-of American poetic theater? It was sexy and funny and mad and high-faluting. James Joyce's *Finnegan's Wake* had bowled over Wilder. Joyce had retold the history of the world in the dream life of an ordinary family and their maid.

Wilder wrote in his journals that he was inspired to write *The Skin of Our Teeth* when a clown hit him with a fish during a performance of *Hellzapoppin'*, an anarchic musical vaudeville carnival that opened on Broadway in 1938 and ran for three years. Clowns ran up and down the aisles hitting audience members with things like fish. Wilder broke the fourth wall, as those clowns and Pirandello had, constantly reminding us we were in a theater. Wilder grafted *Finnegan's Wake* on to *Hellzapoppin'* and filtered it all though his home spun—albeit sophisticated—view of life. Out popped *The Skin of our Teeth*.

Thornton Wilder had written:

"To survive, a story must employ wonder, wonder in both the senses in which we now employ the word: astonishment at the extent of man's capability of good and evil, and speculation as to the sources of that capability."

This sounded the best kind of familiar. Hadn't the great Diaghilev commanded the makers of his ballets: *Etonnez-moi!* Astonish me. Nijinsky and Stravinsky did.

I'd only seen *The Skin of Our Teeth* in a 1955 TV production with Helen Hayes and Mary Martin. They talked into the camera—the world was coming to an end, but man would always manage to survive. Philosophers and dinosaurs came and went. I had seen musicals but I didn't know you could do things like this in a play. I loved it. Sabina continually broke the fourth wall and reminded us we were in a theater. For all its nuttiness, you could understand its success during wartime. We'd survived the Ice Age—the flood—every disaster known to man and we'd survive this nightmare called World War II with our high American spirits intact.

The State Department sent the radiantly positive *The Skin of Our Teeth* on an international tour in 1955 to show off the proper face of America. It's a good face. The play takes place in:

"The home of Mr. George Antrobus, the inventor of the wheel. . . . He comes of very old stock and worked his way up from nothing. . . . Mrs. Antrobus is an excellent needlewoman; it is she who invented the apron on which so many interesting changes have been rung since."

At the end, Mr. Antrobus says: "All I ask is the chance to build new worlds and God has always given us that."

Can you imagine the State Department sending out *Camino Real* as the face of America? "Don't kid yourself. We're all of us guinea pigs in the laboratory of God. Humanity is just a work in progress."

No chance. The people of *Camino Real* were the secrets of America. Where does this play fit in?

Camino Real is the twisted hunchbacked sister to the golden child that is *The Skin of Our Teeth*.

BLOCK ELEVEN
SIDEBAR #2
Bertold Brecht chose *The Skin of Our Teeth* to be the first American play he'd produce at the Berliner Ensemble. I'd love to have seen his take on it.

BLOCK TWELVE
THE BOOK OF JOB
In 1958, another American poetic drama arrived on Broadway with grand credentials, opening at the Yale School of Drama and then going off to the Brussels World's Fair to represent America. It was called *J.B.* The poet Archibald MacLeish retold the Book of Job and cast Job as an American millionaire who lives in a world that is "new and born and fresh and wonderful." It was set in a circus.

J.B. is secure in his faith that God is "just. He'll never change." Then J.B. loses everything in disasters, including Hiroshima. Thanks to his wife, J.B. learns to "blow on the coal of the heart" and restore love and faith in God.

Audiences kept it running for over 300 performances. Like *Skin of our Teeth*, *J.B.* won the Pulitzer Prize and was a best play of the year.

Even at age twenty, I could see this hit was turgid and sentimental and pretentious. MacLeish talked about despair in fancy words but spared us feeling it. That love would inevitably heal everyone in time for the final curtain soaked through every soggy thread of *J.B.* It may be set in a circus but this circus had no high wire acts. No fear of falling here.

Skin. Camino, J.B.—three plays of poetic vision all trying to create a tradition of poetic drama in mainstream America had one thing in common—they all had been directed by Elia Kazan.

BLOCK THIRTEEN
PICK UP THE TORCH
After *J.B.*, Kazan would be one of the founders of the new Repertory Theatre at Lincoln Center which would hopefully mark the creation of an American National Theater. In its first season, Kazan would direct Arthur Miller's *After the Fall* (was this play Miller's *Camino Real*?), followed by Kazan's first foray into classical theater, Middleton's Jacobean tragedy, *The*

Changeling. It received devastatingly bad reviews. Kazan never worked in the theater again.

Kazan had succeeded in refining an acting style for lyrical naturalism in America theater, but he did not succeed in finding a poetic vision.

After *The Skin of Our Teeth*, Thornton Wilder rewrote his failed 1938 farce *The Merchant of Yonkers* based on a 19th-century German play, changed the title to *The Matchmaker* and lived to see it transmogrify into the money machine of *Hello, Dolly!*

Tennessee's next play directed by Kazan would be the lyrical naturalism of *Cat on a Hot Tin Roof.*

MacLeish never wrote another play.

Is the idea of an American poetic theater a torch so diaphanously evanescent that the playwright who tries can only pick it up once and then must move on and trust someone else will carry on the race?

If only *Camino Real* had worked that first time, it might have set American theater, American audiences, on a different journey.

Perhaps time will reveal Kazan's greatest success to have been in his encouraging Tennessee to expand *Ten Blocks* into *Camino Real* and opening the door to a poetic tradition in America.

BLOCK FOURTEEN
LIFE AFTER BROADWAY

But what about *Camino Real*? What kind of life has it had? Has time been good to it?

In 1957, Harold Clurman reported from London on Peter Hall's production:

> "[*Camino Real*] has had its champions, but has not been a popular success. Its direction by Peter Hall has been praised for its color, intriguing stage effects, the movement of its scenes, its heavy application of theatrical detail. All of this is handled with professional skill, but it is an error to confuse these fireworks with creative stage direction.
>
> The material and theme of *Camino Real* have to do with the violence and spiritual depletion of the modern scene: the clamor of heartless entertainment is the most striking ingredient of its atmosphere. But the play—like much of Williams' work—demands a cer-

tain delicacy of tone, a kind of tender hush in which the crudities of action are seen as violations of the over-all benevolence inherent in the dramatist's feeling. A jazz fierceness is not the way to convey Williams' statement. The direction of *Camino Real* 'stands out,' but the melody is lost."

I must add that Clurman had not supported the play in its New York run four years before.

In 1966, PBS, Public Broadcasting, produced *Ten Blocks on the Camino Real* in a charming production with Lotte Lenya as the Gypsy and Martin Sheen as Kilroy. It's available online and worth looking at. You get a taste of the play. But not its visceral presence.

In 1970, *Camino Real* arrived with a thud at Lincoln Center Theater in spite of performances from Al Pacino as Kilroy and no less a light than the original Blanche du Bois, Jessica Tandy, as Marguerite. It was big, elaborate, lifeless, anxiety-free. Pacino and Tandy weren't desperate. They were successes. The audience was successful. It was Broadway all over again. To make this production of *Camino Real* work, the fountain would have had to start bubbling as the plane, *il fugitivo*, returned to pick up all the stragglers left behind. Kilroy would get his golden gloves out of hock, marry the Gypsy's daughter who would go on to invent the apron.

I heard of a production at the Williamstown Theater Festival in 2000 that made the case for the life of *Camino Real*. Ethan Hawke as directed by Nicholas Martin was by all accounts a definitive Kilroy. A projected New York transfer collapsed when Hawke committed to a movie and wasn't available (shades of Brando's involvement). Also the size of the cast made a New York production without a star economically impossible.

Schools do the play quite a bit. It has parts for everyone. But is it possible to do *Camino Real* today? How much of the fault lies with the play itself?

I asked James Leverett who teaches dramaturgy at the Yale School of Drama what was *Camino*'s main problem? He said *Camino Real* has a real trap. "The separateness of the blocks can hold up the dramatic sweep of the play. *Camino* has so many characters that the play can easily lose focus, get swamped in its detail and lose focus."

BLOCK FIFTEEN
BE REALISTIC! DEMAND THE IMPOSSIBLE!

On September 30. 2007, I went to the 2nd Annual Tennessee Williams Festival at Provincetown, Massachusetts. A company of five young actors called Brooklyn on Foot, founded by a young woman named Fayna Sanchez, performed *Camino Real* outdoors on Aquarium Wharf. The performance, directed by Sarah Michelson, began in the afternoon in hot sunshine; by the time we got to Block Fifteen, la Madrecita cries out: "Everyone must see clearly!" It had begun to grow dark. Quixote and Kilroy exited the world of the play, traveling out into the *terra incognita* like Jim and Huck, like Humbert Humbert and Lolita, like Sal Paradise and Dean Moriarty, two uneasy riders off on the great American road trip. The play ended in evening shadows. The bitter cold returned us to an unforgiving reality. And yet we went on. We had been through an experience. We were restored to our old world with new eyes. The Aquarium Wharf became the Globe theater—Tennessee's *teatrum mundi*.

Was it the derring-do, the versatility, the exuberance of the five actors playing all the parts that gave it the focus?

I understood my 1960 rapture with the play. Here on Aquarium Wharf, its spirit welcomed me as electrically as it had forty-seven years before!

Boat traffic coming and going behind the play disintegrated any fourth wall between actors and audience on Aquarium Wharf, and this banishment of the proscenium, made me think of Artaud who wrote In the "Masterpieces" section of *Theatre*, that "it is not upon the stage that the true is to be sought nowadays, but in the street"

Camino Real reminded me of something. Yes—those days in the early 1960s when something called Off-off-Broadway began at places like the Caffé Cino and Café La Mama. That's what the Beat movement had been about, what Ferlinghetti, (echoing Henry Miller) called "a Coney Island of the mind." That was what the Cinema's New Wave was about. That spirit that would find its voice three years later in 1963 with the advent of the Beatles—their nutty extravagant joy—the intoxicating violence of The Rolling Stones who asked "Sympathy for the Devil." When I first heard Bob Dylan's "Desolation Row," I wondered if he knew *Camino Real*. In 1968, the Paris student riots created a new anarchy. One of its famous posters read: "Be realistic. Demand the Impossible." Did *Camino Real*'s rag-tail *joie de vivre* make it a precursor of all this? Was *Camino Real* the harbinger, the John the Baptist, the Big Daddy of this new sensibility?

BLOCK SIXTEEN

A NEW DESTINATION

In 1966, Michael Smith, the Herodotus of this new sensibility, wrote "The Good Scene: Off-off-Broadway" in *The Tulane Drama Review*:

> "Off-off-Broadway is not a place or an idea or a movement or a method or even a group of people. It has no program, no rules, no image to maintain. It is as varied as its participants and they are constantly changing. At its best, it implies a particular point of view: that the procedures of the professional theatre are inadequate; that integrity and the freedom to explore, experiment, and grow count more than respectable or impressive surroundings; that, above all, it is necessary to do the work . . . the real birth of Off-off-Broadway can be dated to September 27, 1960, when Alfred Jarry's *Ubu Roi* opened at the Take 3, a coffee house on Bleecker Street. The program carried the following statement which is still pertinent: "this production . . . represents a return to the original idea of Off-Broadway theatre, in which imagination is substituted for money, and plays can be presented in a way that would be impossible in the commercial theatre."

I loved this detail: note the date of the birth of Off-off-Broadway, Sept 27 1960. While the Yale Dramat was rehearsing its thrilling production of *Camino Real* in New Haven, Off-off-Broadway was being born 75 miles away in Greenwich Village.

Ubu and Camino? That's for another day.

Off-off-Broadway was an American theater of spontaneity and joy and madness—and poetry. I'd see the work of Lanford Wilson, Rosalyn Drexler, Maria Irene Fornes, H.M. Katoukas, Terrence McNally, Paul Foster, Jean-Claude van Itallie, Adrienne Kennedy, Leonard Melfi, Robert Patrick, Rochelle Owens, Robert Heide, Robert Dahdah, Doric Wilson, and Ed Bullins. The plays had a subversive energy. Gay theater was being born here. You couldn't wait to see who'd be playing at La Mama or Caffé Cino or Theater Genesis. Edward Albee ran a playwrights' unit that produced a new play every weekend for six months of the year. A friend of mine called to say he was in a new play called *4-H Club* by this twenty-year-old kid named Sam Shepard. "It's absolutely wonderful. I don't understand a word of it!"

But the most produced playwright at the Caffé Cino was Tennessee Williams. He never went there.

BLOCK SEVENTEEN
HOME?

Tennessee Williams never had a home. He had the typical life of an American playwright. In spite of his Broadway successes, in the last decades of his life no theater would do his new work which would let him grow, sustain him, until the last four years of his life when he became a regular at the Jean Cocteau Repertory Company and the Goodman Theater in Chicago. He made occasional forays back to the world of *Camino* in one-acts like *Slapstick Tragedy* that opened and closed on Broadway. But they didn't belong there!

What would have happened to Tennessee if he could have fit into Off-off-Broadway? The course of an American poetic theater might have taken a different turn.

BLOCK EIGHTEEN
APOLOGIA

As to *Period of Adjustment?* On Christmas day 1960, Tennessee wrote his friend Maria St Just:

> "*Period of Adjustment,* for instance, I thought it was an unimport-ant but charming little play that would be a hit . . . but I should have known better when Kazan suddenly dropped it and sent me a turkey feather before we started rehearsals."

Had Tennessee's agent advised an insecure playwright to toss off a little domestic romantic comedy? How hard can it be? Change your image. Forget cannibalism and rape and castration. Be one of the lovable Broadway gang.

Think of O'Neill's *Ah, Wilderness!* That worked.

Forgive Tennessee his "kinder" and "gentler" play (as he described it to *Newsweek*). Tennessee listened once to those voices—but thank god never again. Remember Esmeralda's prayer:

"God bless . . . the poet who wandered far from his heart's green country and possibly will and possibly won't be able to find his way back . . ."

After straying into alien territory, he found his way back to his heart's green country and never left again. He never had a commercial success after 1961 and *The Night of the Iguana*, but he never stopped writing for the rest of his life. He found his nourishment painting himself into corners he had found in *Camino Real*. The escapes he found in late plays like *The Gnädiges Fräulein, The Two Character Play, A House Not Meant to Stand, In the Bar of a Tokyo Hotel*, and *Something Cloudy, Something Clear* are testaments to a prophet working in the wilderness.

BLOCK NINETEEN
FOR THE EYES OF THE PLAYWRIGHT ONLY

Ibsen kept a portrait of Strindberg over his desk. Ibsen needed those flaming unforgiving eyes of Strindberg's burning into his.

Keep a copy of *Camino Real* by your side. Let it burn into you.

Is it perfect play? Hardly. There may be no such thing as a perfect play (unless it's Calderon's *Life Is A Dream*). *Camino Real* has a very small bull's eye. It's difficult to hit, but when you do, when you do—the world's a brand new place.

Peggy Ramsay the English play agent who guided the careers of Ionesco, Edward Bond, Alan Ayckbourn, Caryl Churchill, David Hare, Vaclav Havel, and Joe Orton advised the young playwright Christopher Hampton after a string of early successes. She said to him, "You can write this play over and over again for the next 40 years, and it'll probably get a little better. Or you can do something completely different." Hampton replied that he was "thinking of writing a play about the extermination of the Brazilian Indians." He said that advice "set my course, really—which was to start again, every time."

Starting again every time.

Experiment.

That's the lesson of *Camino Real*. The way Esmeralda becomes a virgin with each full moon, we have to change the rules of our writing with the new moon of each play.

Why?

This is why. In the early part of that last century, Braque and Picasso realized they could paint as well as anyone ever could. But what would happen if they removed everything they can do. Of course I'm simplifying like crazy, but the point is they did start over and what came up was cubism, a starting point of modernism that gave us a new way of looking at the world. That's the purpose of experimentation. Find new tools. Develop new muscles. See what happens. Why not take the gamble?

And remember that audience for whom you write: the ones who want questions asked and not be given simple answers, the audiences who want the terror, the fear—the ecstasy.

A half century later, I teach that playwriting class at the Yale School of Drama. I've learned to appreciate Ibsen. I've found nourishment in the work of playwrights as diverse as Horton Foote and Joe Orton. But the core is still Tennessee and the voyages he urged us to make and then make again in *Camino Real*. Get lost? We constantly have to keep getting lost on a *Camino Real* of our own making to find a new route to a destination which we hadn't planned.

To learn that the path to that "green country" is through the *Camino Real*—pronounced either way.

Always keep a *Camino Real* in your typewriter, computer, yellow legal pad—whatever you write your plays on—keep working on the impossible play—the play written for the freaks and outlaws, the dreamers without a plan, the fugitives, the desperados, yourselves. Writing for them might not make you the big bucks, but they'll keep you alive.

When *Camino Real* finally opened in London in 1957 Kenneth Tynan wrote:

> "There are three attitudes that a serious writer can adopt towards the world. He can mirror its sickness without comment; he can seek to change it; or he can withdraw from it. Mr. Williams, by recommending withdrawal, places himself in the third batch, along with the saints, the hermits, the junkies and the drunks."

Saint Tennessee, patron saint of the outlaw, the freak, the experimenter, the *fugitivo*? I'd pray to him.

JOHN GUARE
JUNE 2008

FOREWORD*

It is amazing and frightening how completely one's whole being becomes absorbed in the making of a play. It is almost as if you were frantically constructing another world while the world that you live in dissolves beneath your feet, and that your survival depends on completing this construction at least one second before the old habitation collapses.

More than any other work that I have done, this play has seemed to me like the construction of another world, a separate existence. Of course, it is nothing more nor less than my conception of the time and world that I live in, and its people are mostly archetypes of certain basic attitudes and qualities with those mutations that would occur if they had continued along the road to this hypothetical terminal point in it.

A convention of the play is existence outside of time in a place of no specific locality. If you regard it that way, I suppose it becomes an elaborate allegory, but in New Haven we opened directly across the street from a movie theatre that was showing *Peter Pan* in Technicolor and it did not seem altogether inappropriate to me. Fairy tales nearly always have some simple moral lesson of good and evil, but that is not the secret of their fascination any more, I hope, than the philosophical import that might be distilled from the fantasies of *Camino Real* is the principal element of its appeal.

To me the appeal of this work is its unusual degree of freedom. When it began to get under way I felt a new sensation of release, as if I could "ride out" like a tenor sax taking the breaks in a Dixieland combo or a piano in a bop session. You may call it self-indulgence, but I was not doing it merely for myself. I could not have felt a purely private thrill of release unless

---

*Written prior to the Broadway premiere of *Camino Real* and originally published in *The New York Times* on Sunday, March 15, 1953.

I had hope of sharing this experience with lots and lots of audiences to come.

My desire was to give these audiences my own sense of something wild and unrestricted that ran like water in the mountains, or clouds changing shape in a gale, or the continually dissolving and transforming images of a dream. This sort of freedom is not chaos nor anarchy. On the contrary, it is the result of painstaking design, and in this work I have given more conscious attention to form and construction than I have in any work before. Freedom is not achieved simply by working freely.

Elia Kazan was attracted to this work mainly, I believe, for the same reason—its freedom and mobility of form. I know that we have kept saying the word "flight" to each other as if the play were merely an abstraction of the impulse to fly, and most of the work out of town, his in staging, mine in cutting and revising, has been with this impulse in mind: the achievement of a continual flow. Speech after speech and bit after bit that were nice in themselves have been remorselessly blasted out of the script and its staging wherever they seemed to obstruct or divert this flow.

There have been plenty of indications already that this play will exasperate and confuse a certain number of people which we hope is not so large as the number it is likely to please. At each performance a number of people have stamped out of the auditorium, with little regard for those whom they have had to crawl over, almost as if the building had caught on fire, and there have been sibilant noises on the way out and demands for money back if the cashier was foolish enough to remain in his box.

I am at a loss to explain this phenomenon, and if I am being facetious about one thing, I am being quite serious about another when I say that I had never for one minute supposed that the play would seem obscure and confusing to anyone who was willing to meet it even less than halfway. It was a costly production, and for this reason I had to read it aloud, together with a few of the actors on one occasion, before large groups of prospective backers, before the funds to produce it were in the till. It was only then that I came up against the disconcerting surprise that some people would think that the play needed clarification.

My attitude is intransigent. I still don't agree that it needs any explanation. Some poet has said that a poem should not mean but be. Of course, a play is not a poem, not even a poetic play has quite the same license as a poem. But to go to *Camino Real* with the inflexible demands of a logician is unfair to both parties.

In Philadelphia a young man from a literary periodical saw the play and then cross-examined me about all its dreamlike images. He had made a list of them while he watched the play, and afterward at my hotel he brought out the list and asked me to explain the meaning of each one. I can't deny that I use a lot of those things called symbols but being a self-defensive creature, I say that symbols are nothing but the natural speech of drama.

We all have in our conscious and unconscious minds a great vocabulary of images, and I think all human communication is based on these images as are our dreams; and a symbol in a play has only one legitimate purpose which is to say a thing more directly and simply and beautifully than it could be said in words.

I hate writing that is a parade of images for the sake of images; I hate it so much that I close a book in disgust when it keeps on saying one thing is like another; I even get disgusted with poems that make nothing but comparisons between one thing and another. But I repeat that symbols, when used respectfully, are the purest language of plays. Sometimes it would take page after tedious page of exposition to put across an idea that can be said with an object or a gesture on the lighted stage.

To take one case in point: the battered portmanteau of Jacques Casanova is hurled from the balcony of a luxury hotel when his remittance check fails to come through. While the portmanteau is still in the air, he shouts: "Careful, I have—" —and when it has crashed to the street he continues—"fragile—mementos . . .<0x2 01D> I suppose that is a symbol, at least it is an object used to express as directly and vividly as possible certain things which could be said in pages of dull talk.

As for those patrons who departed before the final scene, I offer myself this tentative bit of solace: that these theatregoers may be a little domesticated in their theatrical tastes. A cage represents security as well as confinement to a bird that has grown used to being in it; and when a theatrical work kicks over the traces with such apparent insouciance, security seems challenged and, instead of participating in its sense of freedom, one out of a certain number of playgoers will rush back out to the more accustomed implausibility of the street he lives on.

To modify this effect of complaisance I would like to admit to you quite frankly that I can't say with any personal conviction that I have written a good play, I only know that I have felt a release in this work which I wanted you to feel with me.

TENNESSEE WILLIAMS

AFTERWORD

Once in a while someone will say to me that he would rather wait for a play to come out as a book than see a live performance of it, where he would be distracted from its true values, if it has any, by so much that is mere spectacle and sensation and consequently must be meretricious and vulgar. There are plays meant for reading. I have read them. I have read the works of "thinking playwrights" as distinguished from us who are permitted only to feel, and probably read them earlier and appreciated them as much as those who invoke their names nowadays like the incantation of Aristophanes' frogs. But the incontinent blaze of a live theatre, a theatre meant for seeing and for feeling, has never been and never will be extinguished by a bucket brigade of critics, new or old, bearing vessels that range from cut-glass punch bowl to Haviland teacup. And in my dissident opinion, a play in a book is only the shadow of a play and not even a clear shadow of it. Those who did not like Camino Real on the stage will not be likely to form a higher opinion of it in print, for of all the works I have written, this one was meant most for the vulgarity of performance. The printed script of a play is hardly more than an architect's blueprint of a house not yet built or built and destroyed.

The color, the grace and levitation, the structural pattern in motion, the quick interplay of live beings, suspended like fitful lightning in a cloud, these things are the play, not words on paper, nor thoughts and ideas of an author, those shabby things snatched off basement counters at Gimbel's.

My own creed as a playwright is fairly close to that expressed by the painter in Shaw's play The Doctor's Dilemma: "I believe in Michelangelo,

Velasquez and Rembrandt; in the might of design, the mystery of color, the redemption of all things by beauty everlasting and the message of art that has made these hands blessed. Amen."

How much art his hands were blessed with or how much mine are, I don't know, but that art is a blessing is certain and that it contains its message is also certain, and I feel, as the painter did, that the message lies in those abstract beauties of form and color and line, to which I would add light and motion.

In these following pages are only the formula by which a play could exist.

Dynamic is a word in disrepute at the moment, and so, I suppose, is the word *organic,* but those terms still define the dramatic values that I value most and which I value more as they are more deprecated by the ones self-appointed to save what they have never known.

TENNESSEE WILLIAMS
JUNE 1, 1953

CAMINO REAL

"In the middle of the journey of our life
I came to myself in a dark wood where the
straight way was lost."

CANTO I, DANTE'S *INFERNO*

FOR ELIA KAZAN

EDITOR'S NOTE

The version of *Camino Real* here published is considerably revised over the one presented on Broadway. Following the opening there, Mr. Williams went to his home at Key West and continued to work on this play. When he left six weeks later to direct Donald Windham's *The Starless Air* in Houston, Texas, he took the playing version with him and reworked it whenever time allowed. It was with him when he drove in leisurely fashion back to New York. As delivered to the publisher, the manuscript of *Camino Real* was typed on three different typewriters and on stationery of hotels across the country.

Three characters, a prologue and several scenes that were not in the Broadway production have been added, or reinstated from earlier, preproduction versions, while other scenes have been deleted.

Camino Real is divided into a Prologue and Sixteen "Blocks," scenes with no perceptible time lapse between them for the most part. There are intermissions indicated after Block Six and Block Eleven.

The action takes place in an unspecified Latin-American country.

Camino Real was first produced by Cheryl Crawford and Ethel Reiner, in association with Walter P. Chrysler, Jr., and following tryouts in New Haven and Philadelphia, it had its Broadway premiere on March 19, 1953, at the Martin Beck Theatre. The production was directed by Elia Kazan, with the assistance of Anna Sokolow; the setting and costumes were designed by Lemuel Ayers; and incidental music was contributed by Bernardo Ségall. Production associate: Anderson Lawler. Tennessee Williams was represented by Liebling-Wood.

CAST OF THE ORIGINAL
BROADWAY PRODUCTION

GUTMAN	Frank Silvera
SURVIVOR	Guy Thomajan
ROSITA	Aza Bard
FIRST OFFICER	Henry Silva
JACQUES CASANOVA	Joseph Anthony
LA MADRECITA DE LOS PERDIDOS	Vivian Nathan
HER SON	Rolando Valdez
KILROY	Eli Wallach
FIRST STREETCLEANER	Nehemiah Persoff
SECOND STREETCLEANER	Fred Sadoff
ABDULLAH	Ernesto Gonzalez
A BUM IN A WINDOW	Martin Balsam
A. RATT	Mike Gazzo
THE LOAN SHARK	Salem Ludwig
BARON DE CHARLUS	David J. Stewart
LOBO	Ronne Aul
SECOND OFFICER	William Lennard
A GROTESQUE MUMMER	Gluck Sandor
MARGUERITE GAUTIER	Jo Van Fleet
LADY MULLIGAN	Lucille Patton
WAITER	Page Johnson
LORD BYRON	Hurd Hatfield
NAVIGATOR OF THE FUGITIVO	Antony Vorno
PILOT OF THE FUGITIVO	Martin Balsam
MARKET WOMAN	Charlotte Jones
SECOND MARKET WOMAN	Joanna Vischer
STREET VENDOR	Ruth Volner
LORD MULLIGAN	Parker Wilson
THE GYPSY	Jennie Goldstein
HER DAUGHTER, ESMERALD	Barbara Baxley
NURSIE	Salem Ludwig
EVA	Mary Grey

THE INSTRUCTOR	David J. Stewart
ASSISTANT INSTRUCTOR	Parker Wilson
MEDICAL STUDENT	Page Johnson
DON QUIXOTE	Hurd Hatfield
SANCHO PANZA	*(Not in production)*
PRUDENCE DUVERNOY	*(Not in production)*
OLYMPE	*(Not in production)*

Street Vendors: Aza Bard, Ernesto Gonzalez, Charlotte Jones, Gluck Sandor, Joanna Vischer, Ruth Volner, Antony Vorno.

Guests: Martin Balsam, Mary Grey, Lucille Patton, Joanna Vischer, Parker Wilson.

Passengers: Mike Gazzo, Mary Grey, Page Johnson, Charlotte Jones, William Lennard, Salem Ludwig, Joanna Vischer, Ruth Volner.

At The Fiesta: Ronne Aul, Martin Balsam, Aza Bard, Mike Gazzo, Ernesto Gonzalez, Mary Grey, Charlotte Jones, William Lennard, Nehemiah Persoff, Fred Sadoff, Gluck Sandor, Joanna Vischer, Antony Vorno, Parker Wilson.

PROLOGUE

As the curtain rises, on an almost lightless stage, there is a loud singing of wind, accompanied by distant, measured reverberations like pounding surf or distant shellfire. Above the ancient wall that backs the set and the perimeter of mountains visible above the wall, are flickers of a white radiance as though daybreak were a white bird caught in a net and struggling to rise.

The plaza is seen fitfully by this light. It belongs to a tropical seaport that bears a confusing, but somehow harmonious, resemblance to such widely scattered ports as Tangiers, Havana, Vera Cruz, Casablanca, Shanghai, New Orleans.

On stage left is the luxury side of the street, containing the façade of the Siete Mares Hotel and its low terrace on which are a number of glass-topped white iron tables and chairs. In the downstairs there is a great bay window in which are seen a pair of elegant "dummies," one seated, one standing behind, looking out into the plaza with painted smiles. Upstairs is a small balcony and behind it a large window exposing a wall on which is hung a phoenix painted on silk: this should be softly lighted now and then in the play, since resurrections are so much a part of its meaning.

Opposite the hotel is Skid Row which contains the Gypsy's gaudy stall, the Loan Shark's establishment with a window containing a variety of pawned articles, and the "Ritz Men Only" which is a fleabag hotel or flophouse and which has a practical window above its downstairs entrance, in which a bum will appear from time to time to deliver appropriate or contrapuntal song titles.

Upstage is a great flight of stairs that mount the ancient wall to a sort of archway that leads out into "Terra Incognita," as it is called in the play, a wasteland between the walled town and the distant perimeter of snow-topped mountains.

Downstage right and left are a pair of arches which give entrance to dead-end streets.

Immediately after the curtain rises a shaft of blue light is thrown down a central aisle of the theatre, and in this light, advancing from the back of the house, appears Don Quixote de la Mancha, dressed like an old "desert rat." As he enters the aisle he shouts, "Hola!", in a cracked old voice which is still full of energy and is answered by

5

another voice which is impatient and tired, that of his squire, Sancho
Panza. Stumbling with a fatigue which is only physical, the old knight
comes down the aisle, and Sancho follows a couple of yards behind
him, loaded down with equipment that ranges from a medieval shield
to a military canteen or Thermos bottle. Shouts are exchanged be-
tween them.

QUIXOTE [*ranting above the wind in a voice which is nearly as old*]:
Blue is the color of distance!

SANCHO [*wearily behind him*]: Yes, distance is blue.

QUIXOTE: Blue is also the color of nobility.

SANCHO: Yes, nobility's blue.

QUIXOTE: Blue is the color of distance and nobility, and that's why
an old knight should always have somewhere about him a bit of blue
ribbon . . .

[*He jostles the elbow of an aisle-sitter as he staggers with fatigue;*
he mumbles an apology.]

SANCHO: Yes, a bit of blue ribbon.

QUIXOTE: A bit of faded blue ribbon, tucked away in whatever remains of his armor, or borne on the tip of his lance, his—unconquerable
lance! It serves to remind an old knight of distance that he has gone
and distance he has yet to go . . .

[*Sancho mutters the Spanish word for excrement as several pieces*
of rusty armor fall into the aisle. Quixote has now arrived at the
foot of the steps onto the forestage. He pauses there as if wan-
dering out of or into a dream. Sancho draws up clanging behind
him. Mr. Gutman, a lordly fat man wearing a linen suit and a pith
helmet, appears dimly on the balcony of the Siete Mares, a white
cockatoo on his wrist. The bird cries out harshly.]

GUTMAN: Hush, Aurora.

QUIXOTE: It also reminds an old knight of that green country he
lived in which was the youth of his heart, before such singing words
as *Truth!*

SANCHO [*panting*]: —Truth.

QUIXOTE: *Valor!*

SANCHO: —Valor.

QUIXOTE [*elevating his lance*]: *Devoir!*

SANCHO: —Devoir . . .

QUIXOTE: —turned into the meaningless mumble of some old monk hunched over cold mutton at supper!

[*Gutman alerts a pair of Guards in the plaza, who cross with red lanterns to either side of the proscenium where they lower black and white striped barrier gates as if the proscenium marked a frontier. One of them, with a hand on his holster, advances toward the pair on the steps.*]

GUARD: Vien aquí.

[*Sancho hangs back but Quixote stalks up to the barrier gate. The Guard turns a flashlight on his long and exceedingly grave red face, "frisks" him casually for concealed weapons, examines a rusty old knife and tosses it contemptuously away.*]

Sus papeles! Sus documentos!

[*Quixote fumblingly produces some tattered old papers from the lining of his hat.*]

GUTMAN [*impatiently*]: Who is it?

GUARD: An old desert rat named Quixote.

GUTMAN: Oh!—Expected!—Let him in.

[*The Guards raise the barrier gate and one sits down to smoke on the terrace. Sancho hangs back still. A dispute takes place on the forestage and steps into the aisle.*]

QUIXOTE: Forward!

SANCHO: Aw, naw. I know this place. [*He produces a crumpled parchment.*] Here it is on the chart. Look, it says here: "Continue until you come to the square of a walled town which is the end of the

Ca*mi*no Re*al* and the beginning of the *Ca*mino *Re*al. Halt there," it says, "and turn back, Traveler, for the spring of humanity has gone dry in this place and—"

QUIXOTE [*He snatches the chart from him and reads the rest of the inscription.*]: "—there are no birds in the country except wild birds that are tamed and kept in—" [*He holds the chart close to his nose.*]

—*Cages!*

SANCHO [*urgently*]: Let's go back to La Mancha!

QUIXOTE: Forward!

SANCHO: The time has come for retreat!

QUIXOTE: The time for retreat never comes!

SANCHO: *I'm* going back to *La Mancha!*

[*He dumps the knightly equipment into the orchestra pit.*]

QUIXOTE: *Without me?*

SANCHO [*bustling up the aisle*]: With you or without you, old tireless and tiresome master!

QUIXOTE [*imploringly*]: *Saaaaaan-choooooooooo!*

SANCHO [*near the top of the aisle*]: I'm going back to La Maaaaaaaaan-chaaaaaaa . . .

[*He disappears as the blue light in the aisle dims out. The Guard puts out his cigarette and wanders out of the plaza. The wind moans and Gutman laughs softly as the Ancient Knight enters the plaza with such a desolate air.*]

QUIXOTE [*looking about the plaza*]: —Lonely . . .

[*To his surprise the word is echoed softly by almost unseen figures huddled below the stairs and against the wall of the town. Quixote leans upon his lance and observes with a wry smile—*]

—When so many are lonely as seem to be lonely, it would be inexcusably selfish to be lonely alone.

[*He shakes out a dusty blanket. Shadowy arms extend toward him and voices murmur.*]

VOICE: Sleep. Sleep. Sleep.

QUIXOTE [*arranging his blanket*]: Yes, I'll sleep for a while, I'll sleep and dream for a while against the wall of this town . . .

[*A mandolin or guitar plays "The Nightingale of France."*]

—And my dream will be a pageant, a masque in which old meanings will be remembered and possibly new ones discovered, and when I wake from this sleep and this disturbing pageant of a dream, I'll choose one among its shadows to take along with me in the place of Sancho . . .

[*He blows his nose between his fingers and wipes them on his shirttail.*]

—For new companions are not as familiar as old ones but all the same—they're old ones with only slight differences of face and figure, which may or may not be improvements, and it would be selfish of me to be lonely alone . . .

[*He stumbles down the incline into the Pit below the stairs where most of the Street People huddle beneath awnings of open stalls. The white cockatoo squawks.*]

GUTMAN: Hush, Aurora.

QUIXOTE: And tomorrow at this same hour, which we call madrugada, the loveliest of all words, except the word alba, and that word also means daybreak—

—Yes, at daybreak tomorrow I will go on from here with a new companion and this old bit of blue ribbon to keep me in mind of distance that I have gone and distance I have yet to go, and also to keep me in mind of—

[*The cockatoo cries wildly. Quixote nods as if in agreement with the outcry and folds himself into his blanket below the great stairs.*]

GUTMAN [*stroking the cockatoo's crest*]: Be still, Aurora. I know it's morning, Aurora.

[*Daylight turns the plaza silver and slowly gold. Vendors rise beneath white awnings of stalls. The Gypsy's stall opens. A tall, courtly figure, in his late middle years (Jacques Casanova) crosses from the Siete Mares to the Loan Shark's, removing a silver snuffbox from his pocket as Gutman speaks. His costume, like that of all the legendary characters in the play (except perhaps Quixote) is generally "modern" but with vestigial touches of the period to which he was actually related. The cane and the snuffbox and perhaps a brocaded vest may be sufficient to give this historical suggestion in Casanova's case. He bears his hawklike head with a sort of anxious pride on most occasions, a pride maintained under a steadily mounting pressure.*]

—It's morning and after morning. It's afternoon, ha ha! And now I must go downstairs to announce the beginning of that old wanderer's dream . . .

[*He withdraws from the balcony as old Prudence Duvernoy stumbles out of the hotel, as if not yet quite awake from an afternoon siesta. Chattering with beads and bracelets, she wanders vaguely down into the plaza, raising a faded green silk parasol, damp henna-streaked hair slipping under a monstrous hat of faded silk roses; she is searching for a lost poodle.*]

PRUDENCE: Trique? Trique?

[*Jacques comes out of the Loan Shark's replacing his case angrily in his pocket.*]

JACQUES: Why, I'd rather give it to a street beggar! This case is a Boucheron, I won it at faro at the summer palace, at Tsarskoe Selo in the winter of—

[*The Loan Shark slams the door. Jacques glares, then shrugs and starts across the plaza. Old Prudence is crouched over the filthy gray bundle of a dying mongrel by the fountain.*]

PRUDENCE: Trique, oh, Trique!

[*The Gypsy's son, Abdullah, watches, giggling.*]

JACQUES [*reproving*]: It is a terrible thing for an old woman to outlive her dogs.

[*He crosses to Prudence and gently disengages the animal from her grasp.*]

Madam, that is not Trique.

PRUDENCE: —When I woke up she wasn't in her basket . . .

JACQUES: Sometimes we sleep too long in the afternoon and when we wake we find things changed, Signora.

PRUDENCE: Oh, you're Italian!

JACQUES: I am from Venice, Signora.

PRUDENCE: Ah, Venice, city of pearls! I saw you last night on the terrace dining with—Oh, I'm so worried about her! I'm an old friend of hers, perhaps she's mentioned me to you. Prudence Duvernoy? I was her best friend in the old days in Paris, but now she's forgotten so much . . .

I hope you have influence with her!

[*A waltz of Camille's time in Paris is heard.*]

I want you to give her a message from a certain wealthy old gentleman that she met at one of those watering places she used to go to for her health. She resembled his daughter who died of consumption and so he adored Camille, lavished everything on her! What did she do? Took a young lover who hadn't a couple of pennies to rub together, disinherited by his father because of *her!* Oh, you can't do that, not now, not any more, you've got to be realistic on the Camino Real!

[*Gutman has come out on the terrace: he announces quietly—*]

GUTMAN: Block One on the Camino Real.

PRUDENCE [*continuing*]: Yes, you've got to be practical on it! Well, give her this message, please, Sir. He wants her back on any terms whatsoever! [*Her speech gathers furious momentum.*] Her evenings will be free. He wants only her mornings, mornings are hard on old men because their hearts beat slowly, and he wants only her mornings! Well, that's how it should be! A sensible arrangement! Elderly gentlemen have to content themselves with a lady's spare time before supper! Isn't that so? Of course so! And so I told him! I told him, Camille isn't well! She requires delicate care! Has many debts, creditors storm her door! "How much does she owe?" he asked me, and, oh, did I do some lightning mathematics! Jewels in pawn, I told him, pearls, rings, necklaces, bracelets, diamond eardrops are in pawn! Horses put up for sale at a public auction!

JACQUES [*appalled by this torrent*]: Signora, Signora, all of these things are—

PRUDENCE: —What?

JACQUES: *Dreams!*

[*Gutman laughs. A woman sings at a distance.*]

PRUDENCE [*continuing with less assurance*]: —You're not so young as I thought when I saw you last night on the terrace by candlelight on the—Oh, but—Ho ho!—I bet there is *one* old fountain in this plaza that hasn't gone dry!

[*She pokes him obscenely. He recoils. Gutman laughs. Jacques starts away but she seizes his arm again, and the torrent of speech continues.*]

PRUDENCE: Wait, wait, listen! Her candle is burning low. But how can you tell? She might have a lingering end, and charity hospitals? Why, you might as well take a flying leap into the Streetcleaners' barrel. Oh, I've told her and told her not to live in a dream! A dream is nothing to live in, why, it's gone like a—

Don't let her elegance fool you! That girl has done the Camino in carriages but she has also done it on foot! She knows every stone the

Camino is paved with! So tell her this. You tell her, she won't listen to me!—Times and conditions have undergone certain changes since we were friends in Paris, and now we dismiss young lovers with skins of silk and eyes like a child's first prayer, we put them away as lightly as we put away white gloves meant only for summer, and pick up a pair of black ones, suitable for winter . . .

[*The singing voice rises: then subsides.*]

JACQUES: Excuse me, Madam.

[*He tears himself from her grasp and rushes into the Siete Mares.*]

PRUDENCE [*dazed, to Gutman*]: —What block is this?

GUTMAN: Block One.

PRUDENCE: I didn't hear the announcement . . .

GUTMAN [*coldly*]: Well, now you do.

[*Olympe comes out of the lobby with a pale orange silk parasol like a floating moon.*]

OLYMPE: Oh, there you are, I've looked for you high and low!—mostly low . . .

[*They float vaguely out into the dazzling plaza as though a capricious wind took them, finally drifting through the Moorish arch downstage right. The song dies out.*]

GUTMAN [*lighting a thin cigar*]: Block Two on the Camino Real.

After Gutman's announcement, a hoarse cry is heard. A figure in rags, skin blackened by the sun, tumbles crazily down the steep alley to the plaza. He turns about blindly, murmuring: "A donde la fuente?" He stumbles against the hideous old prostitute Rosita who grins horribly and whispers something to him, hitching up her ragged, filthy shirt. Then she gives him a jocular push toward the fountain. He falls upon his belly and thrusts his hands into the dried-up basin. Then he staggers to his feet with a despairing cry.

THE SURVIVOR: La fuente está seca!

[*Rosita laughs madly but the other Street People moan. A dry gourd rattles.*]

ROSITA: The fountain is dry, but there's plenty to drink in the Siete Mares!

[*She shoves him toward the hotel. The proprietor, Gutman, steps out, smoking a thin cigar, fanning himself with a palm leaf. As the Survivor advances, Gutman whistles. A man in military dress comes out upon the low terrace.*]

OFFICER: Go back!

[*The Survivor stumbles forward. The Officer fires at him. He lowers his hands to his stomach, turns slowly about with a lost expression, looking up at the sky, and stumbles toward the fountain. During the scene that follows, until the entrance of La Madrecita and her Son, the Survivor drags himself slowly about the concrete rim of the fountain, almost entirely ignored, as a dying pariah dog in a starving country. Jacques Casanova comes out upon the terrace of the Siete Mares. Now he passes the hotel proprietor's impassive figure, descending a step beneath and a little in advance of him, and without looking at him.*]

JACQUES [*with infinite weariness and disgust*]: What has happened?

GUTMAN [*serenely*]: We have entered the second in a progress of sixteen blocks on the Camino Real. It's five o'clock. That angry old lion, the Sun, looked back once and growled and then went switching his tail toward the cool shade of the Sierras. Our guests have taken their afternoon siestas . . .

[*The Survivor has come out upon the forestage, now, not like a dying man but like a shy speaker who has forgotten the opening line of his speech. He is only a little crouched over with a hand obscuring the red stain over his belly. Two or three Street People wander about calling their wares: "Tacos, tacos, fritos . . ."—"Loteria, loteria"—Rosita shuffles around, calling "Love? Love?"—pulling down the filthy décolletage of her blouse to show more of her sagging bosom. The Survivor arrives at the top of the stairs descending into the orchestra of the theatre, and hangs onto it, looking out reflectively as a man over the rail of a boat coming into a somewhat disturbingly strange harbor.*]

—They suffer from extreme fatigue, our guests at the Siete Mares, all of them have a degree or two of fever. Questions are passed amongst them like something illicit and shameful, like counterfeit money or drugs or indecent post cards—

[*He leans forward and whispers:*]

—"What is this place? Where are we? What is the meaning of— *Shhhh!*"—Ha ha . . .

THE SURVIVOR [*very softly to the audience*]: I once had a pony named Peeto. He caught in his nostrils the scent of thunderstorms coming even before the clouds had crossed the Sierra . . .

VENDOR: Tacos, tacos, fritos . . .

ROSITA: Love? Love?

LADY MULLIGAN [*to waiter on terrace*]: Are you sure no one called me? I was expecting a call . . .

GUTMAN [*smiling*]: My guests are confused and exhausted but at this hour they pull themselves together, and drift downstairs on the wings of gin and the lift, they drift into the public rooms and exchange notes again on fashionable couturiers and custom tailors, restaurants, vintages of wine, hairdressers, plastic surgeons, girls and young men susceptible to offers . . .

[*There is a hum of light conversation and laughter within.*]

—Hear them? They're exchanging notes . . .

JACQUES [*striking the terrace with his cane*]: I asked you what has happened in the plaza!

GUTMAN: Oh, in the plaza, ha ha!—Happenings in the plaza don't concern us . . .

JACQUES: I heard shots fired.

GUTMAN: Shots were fired to remind you of your good fortune in staying here. The public fountains have gone dry, you know, but the Siete Mares was erected over the only perpetual never-dried-up spring in Tierra Caliente, and of course that advantage has to be—protected—sometimes by—martial law . . .

[*The guitar resumes.*]

THE SURVIVOR: When Peeto, my pony, was born—he stood on his four legs at once, and accepted the world!—He was wiser than I . . .

VENDOR: Fritos, fritos, tacos!

ROSITA: Love!

THE SURVIVOR: —When Peeto was one year old he was wiser than God!

[*A wind sings across the plaza; a dry gourd rattles.*]

"Peeto, Peeto!" the Indian boys call after him, trying to stop him—trying to stop the wind!

[*The Survivor's head sags forward. He sits down as slowly as an old man on a park bench. Jacques strides the terrace again with his cane and starts toward the Survivor. The Guard seizes his elbow.*]

JACQUES: Don't put your hand on *me!*

GUARD: *Stay here.*

GUTMAN: Remain on the terrace, please, Signor Casanova.

JACQUES [*fiercely*]: —*Cognac!*

[*The Waiter whispers to Gutman. Gutman chuckles.*]

GUTMAN: The Maître D' tells me that your credit has been discontinued in the restaurant and bar, he says that he has enough of your tabs to pave the terrace with!

JACQUES: What a piece of impertinence! I told the man that the letter that I'm expecting has been delayed in the mail. The postal service in this country is fantastically disorganized, and you know it! You also know that Mlle. Gautier will guarantee my tabs!

GUTMAN: Then let her pick them up at dinner tonight if you're hungry!

JACQUES: I'm not accustomed to this kind of treatment on the *Camino Real!*

GUTMAN: Oh, you'll be, you'll be, after a single night at the "Ritz Men Only." That's where you'll have to transfer your patronage if the letter containing the remittance check doesn't arrive tonight.

JACQUES: I assure you that I shall do nothing of the sort!—Tonight or ever!

GUTMAN: Watch out, old hawk, the wind is ruffling your feathers!

[*Jacques sinks trembling into a chair.*]

—Give him a thimble of brandy before he collapses . . . Fury is a luxury of the young, their veins are resilient, but his are brittle . . .

JACQUES: Here I sit, submitting to insult for a thimble of brandy— while directly in front of me—

[*The singer, La Madrecita, enters the plaza. She is a blind woman led by a ragged Young Man. The Waiter brings Jacques a brandy.*]

—a man in the plaza dies like a pariah dog!—I take the brandy! I sip it!—My heart is too tired to break, my heart is too tired to—break . . .

[*La Madrecita chants softly. She slowly raises her arm to point at the Survivor crouched on the steps from the plaza.*]

GUTMAN [*suddenly*]: Give me the phone! Connect me with the Palace. Get me the Generalissimo, quick, quick, quick!

[*The Survivor rises feebly and shuffles very slowly toward the extended arms of "The Little Blind One."*]

Generalissimo? Gutman speaking! Hello, sweetheart. There has been a little incident in the plaza. You know that party of young explorers that attempted to cross the desert on foot? Well, one of them's come back. He was very thirsty. He found the fountain dry. He started toward the hotel. He was politely advised to advance no further. But he disregarded this advice. Action had to be taken. And now, and now—that old blind woman they call "La Madrecita"?—She's come into the plaza with the man called "The Dreamer" . . .

SURVIVOR: Donde?

THE DREAMER: Aquí!

GUTMAN [*continuing*]: You remember those two! I once mentioned them to you. You said "They're harmless dreamers and they're loved by the people."—"What," I asked you, "is harmless about a dreamer, and what," I asked you, "is harmless about the love of the people?—Revolution only needs good dreamers who remember their dreams, and the love of the people belongs safely only to you—their Generalissimo!"—Yes, now the blind woman has recovered her sight and is extending her arms to the wounded Survivor, and the man with the guitar is leading him to her . . .

[*The described action is being enacted.*]

Wait one moment! There's a possibility that the forbidden word may be spoken! Yes! The forbidden word is about to be spoken!

[*The Dreamer places an arm about the blinded Survivor, and cries out:*]

THE DREAMER: *Hermano!*

[*The cry is repeated like springing fire and a loud murmur sweeps the crowd. They push forward with cupped hands extended and the gasping cries of starving people at the sight of bread. Two Military Guards herd them back under the colonnades with clubs and*

*drawn revolvers. La Madrecita chants softly with her blind eyes
lifted. A Guard starts toward her. The People shout "NO!"*]

LA MADRECITA [*chanting*]: "Rojo está el sol! Rojo está el sol de
sangre! Blanca está la luna! Blanca está la luna de miedo!"

[*The crowd makes a turning motion.*]

GUTMAN [*to the waiter*]: Put up the ropes!

[*Velvet ropes are strung very quickly about the terrace of the Siete
Mares. They are like the ropes on decks of steamers in rough waters. Gutman shouts into the phone again:*]

The word was spoken. The crowd is agitated. Hang on! [*He lays
down instrument.*]

JACQUES [*hoarsely, shaken*]: He said "Hermano." That's the word
for brother.

GUTMAN [*calmly*]: Yes, the most dangerous word in any human
tongue is the word for brother. It's inflammatory.—I don't suppose it
can be struck out of the language altogether but it must be reserved
for strictly private usage in back of soundproof walls. Otherwise it
disturbs the population . . .

JACQUES: The people need the word. They're thirsty for it!

GUTMAN: What are these creatures? Mendicants. Prostitutes.
Thieves and petty vendors in a bazaar where the human heart is a
part of the bargain.

JACQUES: Because they need the word and the word is forbidden!

GUTMAN: The word is said in pulpits and at tables of council where
its volatile essence can be contained. But on the lips of these creatures,
what is it? A wanton incitement to riot, without understanding. For
what is a brother to them but someone to get ahead of, to cheat, to lie
to, to undersell in the market. Brother, you say to a man whose wife
you sleep with!—But now, you see, the word has disturbed the people
and made it necessary to invoke martial law!

[*Meanwhile the Dreamer has brought the Survivor to La Madrecita, who is seated on the cement rim of the fountain. She has*]

cradled the dying man in her arms in the attitude of a Pietà. The Dreamer is crouched beside them, softly playing a guitar. Now he springs up with a harsh cry:]

THE DREAMER: *Muerto!*

[*The Streetcleaners' piping commences at a distance. Gutman seizes the phone again.*]

GUTMAN [*into phone*]: Generalissimo, the Survivor is no longer surviving. I think we'd better have some public diversion right away. Put the Gypsy on! Have her announce the Fiesta!

LOUDSPEAKER [*responding instantly*]: Damas y Caballeros! The next voice you hear will be the voice of—the Gypsy!

GYPSY [*over loudspeaker*]: Hoy! Noche de Fiesta! Tonight the moon will restore the virginity of my daughter!

GUTMAN: Bring on the Gypsy's daughter, Esmeralda. Show the virgin-to-be!

[*Esmeralda is led from the Gypsy's stall by a severe duenna, "Nursie," out upon the forestage. She is manacled by the wrist to the duenna. Her costume is vaguely Levantine. Guards are herding the crowd back again.*]

GUTMAN: Ha ha! Ho ho ho! Music!

[*There is gay music. Rosita dances.*]

Abdullah! You're on!

[*Abdullah skips into the plaza, shouting histrionically.*]

ABDULLAH: Tonight the moon will restore the virginity of my sister, Esmeralda!

GUTMAN: *Dance, boy!*

[*Esmeralda is led back into the stall. Throwing off his burnoose, Abdullah dances with Rosita. Behind their dance, armed Guards force La Madrecita and the Dreamer to retreat from the fountain, leaving the lifeless body of the Survivor. All at once there is a discordant blast of brass instruments.*]

[*Kilroy comes into the plaza. He is a young American vagrant, about twenty-seven. He wears dungarees and a skivvy shirt, the pants faded nearly white from long wear and much washing, fitting him as closely as the clothes of sculpture. He has a pair of golden boxing gloves slung about his neck and he carries a small duffle bag. His belt is ruby-and-emerald-studded with the word CHAMP in bold letters. He stops before a chalked inscription on a wall downstage which says: "Kilroy Is Coming!" He scratches out "Coming" and over it prints "Here!"*]

GUTMAN: Ho ho!—a clown! The Eternal Punchinella! That's exactly what's needed in a time of crisis!

Block Three on the Camino Real.

KILROY [*genially, to all present*]: Ha ha!

[*Then he walks up to the Officer by the terrace of the Siete Mares.*]

Buenas dias, señor.

[*He gets no response—barely even a glance.*]

Habla Inglesia? Usted?

OFFICER: What is it you want?

KILROY: Where is Western Union or Wells-Fargo? I got to send a wire to some friends in the States.

OFFICER: No hay Western Union, no hay Wells-Fargo.

KILROY: That is very peculiar. I never struck a town yet that didn't have one or the other. I just got off a boat. Lousiest frigging tub I ever shipped on, one continual hell it was, all the way up from Rio. And me sick, too. I picked up one of those tropical fevers. No sick bay on that tub, no doctor, no medicine or nothing, not even one quinine pill, and I was burning up with Christ knows how much fever. I couldn't make them understand I was sick. I got a bad heart, too. I had to retire from the prize ring because of my heart. I was the light heavyweight champion of the West Coast, won these gloves!—before my ticker went bad.—Feel my chest! Go on, feel it! Feel it. I've got a heart in my chest as big as the head of a baby. Ha ha! They stood me in front of a screen that makes you transparent and that's what they seen inside me, a heart in my chest as big as the head of a baby! With something like that you don't need the Gypsy to tell you, "Time is short, Baby—get ready to hitch on wings!" The medics wouldn't okay me for no more fights. They said to give up liquor and smoking and sex!—To give up sex!—I used to believe a man couldn't live without sex—but he can—if he wants to! My real true woman, my wife, she would of stuck with me, but it was all spoiled with her being scared and me, too, that a real hard kiss would kill me!—So one night while she was sleeping I wrote her good-bye . . .

[*He notices a lack of attention in the Officer: he grins.*]

No comprendo the lingo?

OFFICER: What is it you want?

KILROY: Excuse my ignorance, but what place is this? What is this country and what is the name of this town? I know it seems funny of me to ask such a question. Loco! But I was so glad to get off that rotten tub that I didn't ask nothing of no one except my pay—and I got shortchanged on that. I have trouble counting these pesos or Whatzit-you-call-'em. [*He jerks out his wallet.*] All-a-this-here. In the States that pile of lettuce would make you a plutocrat!—But I bet you this stuff don't add up to fifty dollars American coin. Ha ha!

OFFICER: Ha ha.

KILROY: Ha ha!

OFFICER [*making it sound like a death rattle*]: Ha-ha-ha-ha-ha.

[*He turns and starts into the cantina. Kilroy grabs his arm.*]

KILROY: Hey!

OFFICER: What is it you want?

KILROY: What is the name of this country and this town?

[*The Officer thrusts his elbow in Kilroy's stomach and twists his arm loose with a Spanish curse. He kicks the swinging doors open and enters the cantina.*]

Brass hats are the same everywhere.

[*As soon as the Officer goes, the Street People come forward and crowd about Kilroy with their wheedling cries.*]

STREET PEOPLE: Dulces, dulces! Lotería! Lotería! Pasteles, café con leche!

KILROY: No caree, no caree!

[*The Prostitute creeps up to him and grins.*]

ROSITA: Love? Love?

KILROY: What did you say?

24

ROSITA: *Love?*

KILROY: Sorry—I don't feature that, [*to audience*] I have ideals.

[*The Gypsy appears on the roof of her establishment with Esmeralda whom she secures by handcuffs to the iron railing.*]

GYPSY: Stay there while I give the pitch!

[*She then advances with a portable microphone.*]

Testing! One, two, three, four!

NURSIE [*from offstage*]: You're on the air!

GYPSY'S LOUDSPEAKER: Are you perplexed by something? Are you tired out and confused? Do you have a fever?

[*Kilroy look around for the source of the voice.*]

Do you feel yourself to be spiritually unprepared for the age of exploding atoms? Do you distrust the newspapers? Are you suspicious of governments? Have you arrived at a point on the Camino Real where the walls converge not in the distance but right in front of your nose? Does further progress appear impossible to you? Are you afraid of anything at all? Afraid of your heartbeat? Or the eyes of strangers! Afraid of breathing? Afraid of not breathing? Do you wish that things could be straight and simple again as they were in your childhood? Would you like to go back to Kindy Garten?

[*Rosita has crept up to Kilroy while he listens. She reaches out to him. At the same time a Pickpocket lifts his wallet.*]

KILROY [*catching the whore's wrist*]: Keep y'r hands off me, y' dirty ole bag! No caree putas! No loteria, no dulces, nada—so get away! Vamoose! All of you! Quit picking at me!

[*He reaches in his pocket and jerks out a handful of small copper and silver coins which he flings disgustedly down the street. The grotesque people scramble after it with their inhuman cries. Kilroy goes on a few steps—then stops short—feeling the back pocket of his dungarees. Then he lets out a startled cry.*]

Robbed! My God, I've been robbed!

[*The Street People scatter to the walls.*]

Which of you got my wallet? *Which* of you dirty—? Shh-Uh!

[*They mumble with gestures of incomprehension. He marches back to the entrance to the hotel.*]

Hey! Officer! Official!—General!

[*The Officer finally lounges out of the hotel entrance and glances at Kilroy.*]

Tiende? One of them's got my wallet! Picked it out of my pocket while that old whore there was groping me! Don't you comprendo?

OFFICER: Nobody rob you. You don't have no pesos.

KILROY: Huh?

OFFICER: You just dreaming that you have money. You don't ever have money. Nunca! Nada! [*He spits between his teeth.*] Loco . . . [*The Officer crosses to the fountain. Kilroy stares at him, then bawls out:*]

KILROY [*to the Street People*]: We'll see what the American Embassy has to say about this! I'll go to the American Consul. Whichever of you rotten spivs lifted my wallet is going to jail—calaboose! I hope I have made myself plain. If not, I will make myself plainer!

[*There are scattered laughs among the crowd. He crosses to the fountain. He notices the body of the no longer Survivor, kneels beside it, shades it, turns it over, springs up and shouts:*]

Hey! This guy is dead!

[*There is the sound of the Streetcleaners' piping. They trundle their white barrel into the plaza from one of the downstage arches. The appearance of these men undergoes a progressive alteration through the play. When they first appear they are almost like any such public servants in a tropical country; their white jackets are dirtier than the musicians' and some of the stains are red. They have on white caps with black visors. They are continually exchanging sly jokes and giggling unpleasantly together. Lord Mulligan has come out upon the terrace and as they pass him, they pause for a moment, point at him, snicker. He is extremely discomfited by this impertinence, touches his chest as if he felt a palpitation and turns back inside. Kilroy yells to the advancing Streetcleaners.*]

There's a dead man layin' here!

[*They giggle again. Briskly they lift the body and stuff it into the barrel; then trundle it off, looking back at Kilroy, giggling, whispering. They return under the downstage arch through which they entered. Kilroy, in a low, shocked voice:*] What *is* this place? What kind of a hassle have I got myself into?

LOUDSPEAKER: If anyone on the Camino is bewildered, come to the Gypsy. A poco dinero will tickle the Gypsy's palm and give her visions!

ABDULLAH [*giving Kilroy a card*]: If you got a question, ask my mama, the Gypsy!

KILROY: Man, whenever you see those three brass balls on a street, you don't have to look a long ways for a Gypsy. Now let me think. I am faced with three problems. One: I'm hungry. Two: I'm lonely. Three: I'm in a place where I don't know what it is or how I got there! First action that's indicated is to—cash in on something—Well . . . let's see . . .

[*Honky-tonk music fades in at this point and the Skid Row façade begins to light up for the evening. There is the Gypsy's stall with its cabalistic devices, its sectional cranium and palm, three luminous brass balls overhanging the entrance to the Loan Shark and his window filled with a vast assortment of hocked articles for sale: trumpets, banjos, fur coats, tuxedos, a gown of scarlet sequins, loops of pearls and rhinestones. Dimly behind this display is a neon sign in three pastel colors, pink, green, and blue. It fades softly in and out and it says: "Magic Tricks Jokes." There is also the advertisement of a flea-bag hotel or flophouse called "Ritz Men Only." This sign is also pale neon or luminous paint, and only the entrance is on the street floor, the rooms are above the Loan Shark and Gypsy's stall. One of the windows of this upper story is practical. Figures appear in it sometimes, leaning out as if suffocating or to hawk and spit into the street below. This side of the street should have all the color and animation that are permitted by the resources of the production. There may be moments of dancelike action (a fight, a seduction, sale of narcotics, arrest, etc.).*]

27

KILROY [*to the audience from the apron*]: What've I got to cash in on? My golden gloves? Never! I'll say that once more, never! The silver-framed photo of my One True Woman? Never! Repeat that! Never! What else have I got of a detachable and a negotiable nature? Oh! My ruby-and-emerald-studded belt with the word CHAMP on it.

[*He whips it off his pants.*]

This is not necessary to hold on my pants, but this is a precious reminder of the sweet used-to-be. Oh, well. Sometimes a man has got to hock his sweet used-to-be in order to finance his present situation . . .

[*He enters the Loan Shark's. A Drunken Bum leans out the practical window of the "Ritz Men Only" and shouts:*]

BUM: O Jack o' Diamonds, you robbed my pockets, you robbed my pockets of silver and gold!

[*He jerks the window shade down.*]

GUTMAN [*on the terrace*]: Block Four on the Camino Real!

BLOCK FOUR

There is a phrase of light music as the Baron de Charlus, an elderly foppish sybarite in a light silk suit, a carnation in his lapel, crosses from the Siete Mares to the honky-tonk side of the street. On his trail is a wild-looking young man of startling beauty called Lobo. Charlus is aware of the follower and, during his conversation with A. Ratt, he takes out a pocket mirror to inspect him while pretending to comb his hair and point his moustache. As Charlus approaches, the Manager of the flea-bag puts up a vacancy sign and calls out:

A. RATT: Vacancy here! A bed at the "Ritz Men Only"! A little white ship to sail the dangerous night in . . .

THE BARON: Ah, bon soir, Mr. Ratt.

A. RATT: Cruising?

THE BARON: No, just—walking!

A. RATT: That's all you need to do.

THE BARON: I sometimes find it suffices. You have a vacancy, do you?

A. RATT: For you?

THE BARON: And a possible guest. You know the requirements. An iron bed with no mattress and a considerable length of stout knotted rope. No! Chains this evening, metal chains. I've been very bad, I have a lot to atone for . . .

A. RATT: Why don't you take these joy rides at the Siete Mares?

THE BARON [*with the mirror focused on Lobo*]: They don't have Ingreso Libero at the Siete Mares. Oh, I don't like places in the haute saison, the alta staggione, and yet if you go between the fashionable seasons, it's too hot or too damp or appallingly overrun by all the wrong sort of people who rap on the wall if canaries sing in your bedsprings after midnight. I don't know why such people don't stay at home. Surely a Kodak, a Brownie, or even a Leica works just as well in Milwaukee or Sioux City as it does in these places they do on their whirlwind summer tours, and don't look now, but I think I am being followed!

A. RATT: Yep, you've made a pickup!

THE BARON: Attractive?

A. RATT: That depends on who's driving the bicycle, Dad.

THE BARON: Ciao, Caro! Expect me at ten.

[*He crosses elegantly to the fountain.*]

A. RATT: Vacancy here! A little white ship to sail the dangerous night in!

[*The music changes. Kilroy backs out of the Loan Shark's, belt unsold, engaged in a violent dispute. The Loan Shark is haggling for his golden gloves. Charlus lingers, intrigued by the scene.*]

LOAN SHARK: I don't want no belt! I want the gloves! Eight-fifty!

KILROY: No dice.

LOAN SHARK: Nine, nine-fifty!

KILROY: Nah, nah, nah!

LOAN SHARK: Yah, yah, yah.

KILROY: I say nah.

LOAN SHARK: I say yah.

KILROY: The nahs have it.

LOAN SHARK: Don't be a fool. What can you do with a pair of golden gloves?

KILROY: I can remember the battles I fought to win them! I can remember that I used to be—CHAMP!

[*Fade in Band Music: "March of the Gladiators"—ghostly cheers, etc.*]

LOAN SHARK: You can remember that you *used to be*—Champ?

KILROY: Yes! I used to be—CHAMP!

THE BARON: Used to be is the past tense, meaning useless.

KILROY: Not to me, Mister. These are my gloves, these gloves are gold, and I fought a lot of hard fights to win 'em! I broke clean from the clinches. I never hit a low blow, the referee never told me to mix it up! And the fixers never got to me!

LOAN SHARK: In other words, a sucker!

KILROY: Yep, I'm a sucker that won the golden gloves!

LOAN SHARK: Congratulations. My final offer is a piece of green paper with Alexander Hamilton's picture on it. Take it or leave it.

KILROY: I leave it for you to *stuff* it! I'd hustle my heart on this street, I'd peddle my heart's true blood before I'd leave my golden gloves hung up in a loan shark's window between a rusted trombone and some poor lush's long-ago mildewed tuxedo!

LOAN SHARK: So you say but I will see you later.

THE BARON: The name of the Camino is not unreal!

[*The Bum sticks his head out the window and shouts:*]

BUM: Pa dam, Pa dam, Pa dam!

THE BARON [*continuing the Bum's song*]: Echoes the beat of my heart! Pa dam, Pa dam—*hello!*

[*He has crossed to Kilroy as he sings and extends his hand to him.*]

KILROY [*uncertainly*]: Hey, mate. It's wonderful to see you.

THE BARON: Thanks, but why?

KILROY: A normal American. In a clean white suit.

THE BARON: My suit is pale yellow. My nationality is French, and my normality has been often subject to question.

KILROY: I still say your suit is clean.

THE BARON: Thanks. That's more than I can say for your apparel.

KILROY: Don't judge a book by the covers. I'd take a shower if I could locate the "Y."

THE BARON: What's the "Y"?

KILROY: Sort of a Protestant church with a swimmin' pool in it. Sometimes it also has an employment bureau. It does good in the community.

THE BARON: Nothing in this community does much good.

KILROY: I'm getting the same impression. This place is confusing to me. I think it must be the aftereffects of fever. Nothing seems real. Could you give me the scoop?

THE BARON: Serious questions are referred to the Gypsy. Once upon a time. Oh, once upon a time. I used to wonder. Now I simply wander. I stroll about the fountain and hope to be followed. Some people call it corruption. I call it—simplification . . .

BUM [very softly at the window]: I wonder what's become of Sally, that old gal of mine?

[He lowers the blind.]

KILROY: Well, anyhow . . .

THE BARON: Well, anyhow?

KILROY: How about the hot-spots in this town?

THE BARON: Oh, the hot spots, ho ho! There's the Pink Flamingo, the Yellow Pelican, the Blue Heron, and the Prothonotary Warbler! They call it the Bird Circuit. But I don't care for such places. They stand three-deep at the bar and look at themselves in the mirror and what they see is depressing. One sailor comes in—they faint! My own choice of resorts is the Bucket of Blood downstairs from the "Ritz Men Only."— How about a match?

KILROY: Where's your cigarette?

THE BARON [gently and sweetly]: Oh, I don't smoke. I just wanted to see your eyes more clearly . . .

KILROY: Why?

THE BARON: The eyes are the windows of the soul, and yours are too gentle for someone who has as much as I have to atone for.

[*He starts off.*]

Au revoir . . .

KILROY: —A very unusual type character . . .

[*Casanova is on the steps leading to the arch, looking out at the desert beyond. Now he turns and descends a few steps, laughing with a note of tired incredulity. Kilroy crosses to him.*]

Gee, it's wonderful to see you, a normal American in a—

[*There is a strangulated outcry from the arch under which the Baron has disappeared.*]

Excuse me a minute!

[*He rushes toward the source of the outcry. Jacques crosses to the bench before the fountain. Rhubarb is heard through the arch. Jacques shrugs wearily as if it were just a noisy radio. Kilroy comes plummeting out backward, all the way to Jacques.*]

I tried to interfere, but what's th' use?!

JACQUES: No use at all!

[*The Streetcleaners come through the arch with the Baron doubled up in their barrel. They pause and exchange sibilant whispers, pointing and snickering at Kilroy.*]

KILROY: Who are they pointing at? At me, Kilroy?

[*The Bum laughs from the window. A. Ratt laughs from his shadowy doorway. The Loan Shark laughs from his.*]

Kilroy is here and he's not about to be there!—If he can help it . . .

[*He snatches up a rock and throws it at the Streetcleaners. Everybody laughs louder and the laughter seems to reverberate from the mountains. The light changes, dims a little in the plaza.*]

Sons a whatever you're sons of! Don't look at me, I'm not about to take no ride in the barrel!

[*The Baron, his elegant white shoes protruding from the barrel, is wheeled up the Alleyway Out. Figures in the square resume their dazed attitudes and one or two Guests return to the terrace of the Siete Mares as—*]

GUTMAN: Block Five on the Camino Real!

[*He strolls off.*]

KILROY [*to Jacques*]: Gee, the blocks go fast on this street!

JACQUES: Yes. The blocks go fast.

KILROY: My name's Kilroy. I'm here.

JACQUES: Mine is Casanova. I'm here, too.

KILROY: But you been here longer than me and maybe could brief me on it. For instance, what do they do with a stiff picked up in this town?

[*The Guard stares at them suspiciously from the terrace. Jacques whistles "La Golondrina" and crosses downstage. Kilroy follows.*]

Did I say something untactful?

JACQUES [*smiling into a sunset glow*]: The exchange of serious questions and ideas, especially between persons from opposite sides of the plaza, is regarded unfavorably here. You'll notice I'm talking as if I had acute laryngitis. I'm gazing into the sunset. If I should start to whistle "La Golondrina" it means we're being overheard by the Guards on the terrace. Now you want to know what is done to a body from which the soul has departed on the Camino Real!—Its disposition depends on what the Streetcleaners happen to find in its pockets. If its pockets are empty as the unfortunate Baron's turned out to be, and as mine are at this moment—the "stiff" is wheeled straight off to the Laboratory. And there the individual becomes an undistinguished member of a collectivist state. His chemical components are separated and poured into vats containing the corresponding elements of countless others. If any of his vital organs or parts are at all unique in size or structure, they're placed on exhibition in bottles containing a very foul-smelling solution called formaldehyde. There is a charge of admission to this museum. The proceeds go to the maintenance of the military police.

[*He whistles "La Golondrina" till the Guard turns his back again. He moves toward the front of the stage.*]

KILROY [*following*]: —I guess that's—sensible . . .

JACQUES: Yes, but not romantic. And romance is important. Don't you think?

KILROY: Nobody thinks romance is more important than me!

JACQUES: Except possibly me!

KILROY: Maybe that's why fate has brung us together! We're buddies under the skin!

JACQUES: Travelers born?

KILROY: Always looking for something!

JACQUES: Satisfied by nothing!

KILROY: Hopeful?

JACQUES: Always!

OFFICER: Keep moving!

[*They move apart till the Officer exits.*]

KILROY: And when a joker on the Camino gets fed up with one continual hassle—how does he get *off* it?

JACQUES: You see the narrow and very steep stairway that passes under what is described in the travel brochures as a "Magnificent Arch of Triumph"?—Well, that's the Way Out!

KILROY: That's the way out?

[*Kilroy without hesitation plunges right up to almost the top step; then pauses with a sound of squealing brakes. There is a sudden loud wind.*]

JACQUES [*shouting with hand cupped to mouth*]: Well, how does the prospect please you, Traveler born?

KILROY [*shouting back in a tone of awe*]: It's too unknown for my blood. Man, I seen nothing like it except through a telescope once on the pier on Coney Island. "Ten cents to see the craters and plains of the moon!"—And here's the same view in three dimensions for nothing!

[*The desert wind sings loudly: Kilroy mocks it.*]

JACQUES: Are you—ready to cross it?

KILROY: Maybe sometime with someone but not right now and alone! How about you?

JACQUES: I'm not alone.

KILROY: You're with a party?

JACQUES: No, but I'm sweetly encumbered with a—lady . . .

KILROY: It wouldn't do with a lady. I don't see nothing but nothing—and then more nothing. And then I see some mountains. But the mountains are covered with snow.

JACQUES: Snowshoes would be useful!

[*He observes Gutman approaching through the passage at upper left. He whistles "La Golondrina" for Kilroy's attention and points with his cane as he exits.*]

KILROY [*descending steps disconsolately*]: Mush, mush.

[*The Bum comes to his window. A. Ratt enters his doorway. Gutman enters below Kilroy.*]

BUM: It's sleepy time down South!

GUTMAN [*warningly as Kilroy passes him*]: Block Six in a progress of sixteen blocks on the Camino Real.

KILROY [*from the stairs*]: Man, I could use a bed now.—I'd like to make me a cool pad on this camino now and lie down and sleep and dream of being with someone—friendly . . .

[*He crosses to the "Ritz Men Only."*]

A. RATT [*softly and sleepily*]: Vacancy here! I got a single bed at the "Ritz Men Only," a little white ship to sail the dangerous night in.

[*Kilroy crosses down to his doorway.*]

KILROY: —You got a vacancy here?

A. RATT: I got a vacancy here if you got the one-fifty there.

KILROY: Ha ha! I been in countries where money was not legal tender. I mean it was legal but it wasn't tender.

[*There is a loud groan from offstage above.*]

—Somebody dying on you or just drunk?

A. RATT: Who knows or cares in this pad, Dad?

KILROY: I heard once that a man can't die while he's drunk. Is that a fact or a fiction?

A. RATT: Strictly a fiction.

VOICE ABOVE: *Stiff in number seven! Call the Streetcleaners!*

A. RATT [*with absolutely no change in face or voice*]: Number seven is vacant.

[*Streetcleaners' piping is heard. The Bum leaves the window.*]

KILROY: Thanks, but tonight I'm going to sleep under the stars.

[*A. Ratt gestures "Have it your way" and exits. Kilroy, left alone, starts downstage. He notices that La Madrecita is crouched near the fountain, holding something up, inconspicuously, in her hand. Coming to her he sees that it's a piece of food. He takes it, puts it in his mouth, tries to thank her but her head is down, muffled in her rebozo and there is no way for him to acknowledge the gift.*]

He starts to cross. Street People raise up their heads in their Pit and motion him invitingly to come in with them. They call softly, "Sleep, sleep . . ."]

GUTMAN [*from his chair on the terrace*]: Hey, Joe.

[*The Street People duck immediately.*]

KILROY: Who? Me?

GUTMAN: Yes, you, Candy Man. Are you disocupado?

KILROY: —That means—unemployed, don't it?

[*He sees Officers converging from right.*]

GUTMAN: Jobless. On the bum. Carrying the banner!

KILROY: —Aw, no, aw, no, don't try to hang no vagrancy rap on me! I was robbed on this square and I got plenty of witnesses to prove it.

GUTMAN [*with ironic courtesy*]: Oh?

[*He makes a gesture asking "Where?"*]

KILROY [*coming down to apron left and crossing to the right*]: Witnesses! Witness! Witnesses! [*He comes to La Madrecita.*]

You were a witness!

[*A gesture indicates that he realizes her blindness. Opposite the Gypsy's balcony he pauses for a second.*]

Hey, Gypsy's daughter!

[*The balcony is dark. He continues up to the Pit. The Street People duck as he calls down:*]

You were witnesses!

[*An Officer enters with a Patsy outfit. He hands it to Gutman.*]

GUTMAN: Here, Boy! Take these.

[*Gutman displays and then tosses on the ground at Kilroy's feet the Patsy outfit—the red fright wig, the big crimson nose that lights up and has horn-rimmed glasses attached, a pair of clown pants that have a huge footprint on the seat.*]

KILROY: What is this outfit?

GUTMAN: The uniform of a Patsy.

KILROY: I know what a Patsy is—he's a clown in the circus who takes pratfalls *but I'm no Patsy!*

GUTMAN: Pick it up.

KILROY: Don't give me orders. Kilroy is a free agent—

GUTMAN [*smoothly*]: But a Patsy isn't. Pick it up and put it on, Candy Man. You are now the Patsy.

KILROY: So you say but you are completely mistaken.

[*Four Officers press in on him.*]

And don't crowd me with your torpedoes! I'm a stranger here but I got a clean record in all the places I been, I'm not in the books for nothin' but vagrancy and once when I was hungry I walked by a truck-load of pineapples without picking one, because I was brought up good—

[*Then, with a pathetic attempt at making friends with the Officer to his right.*]

and there was a cop on the corner!

OFFICER: Ponga selo!

KILROY: What'd you say?

[*Desperately to audience he asks:*]

What did he say?

OFFICER: Ponga selo!

KILROY: What'd you say?

[*The Officer shoves him down roughly to the Patsy outfit. Kilroy picks up the pants, shakes them out carefully as if about to step into them and says very politely:*]

Why, surely. I'd be delighted. My fondest dreams have come true.

[*Suddenly he tosses the Patsy dress into Gutman's face and leaps into the aisle of the theatre.*]

GUTMAN: Stop him! Arrest that vagrant! Don't let him get away!

LOUDSPEAKER: Be on the lookout for a fugitive Patsy. The Patsy has escaped. Stop him, stop that Patsy!

[*A wild chase commences. The two Guards rush madly down either side to intercept him at the back of the house. Kilroy wheels about at the top of the center aisle, and runs back down it, panting, gasping out questions and entreaties to various persons occupying aisle seats, such as:*]

KILROY: How do I git out? Which way do I go, which way do I get out? Where's the Greyhound depot? Hey, do you know where the Greyhound bus depot is? What's the best way out, if there is any way out? I got to find one. I had enough of this place. I had too much of this place. I'm free. I'm a free man with equal rights in this world! You better believe it because that's news for you and you had better believe it! Kilroy's a free man with equal rights in this world! All right, now, help me, somebody, help me find a way out, I got to find one, I don't like this place! It's not for me and I am not buying any! Oh! Over there! I see a sign that says EXIT. That's a sweet word to me, man, that's a lovely word, EXIT! That's the entrance to paradise for Kilroy! Exit, I'm coming, Exit, I'm coming!

[*The Street People have gathered along the forestage to watch the chase. Esmeralda, barefooted, wearing only a slip, bursts out of the Gypsy's establishment like an animal broken out of a cage, darts among the Street People to the front of the crowd which is shouting like the spectators at the climax of a corrida. Behind her, Nursie appears, a male actor, wigged and dressed austerely as a duenna, crying out in both languages.*]

NURSIE: Esmeralda! Esmeralda!

GYPSY: Police!

NURSIE: Come back here, Esmeralda!

GYPSY: Catch her, idiot!

NURSIE: Where is my lady bird, where is my precious treasure?

GYPSY: Idiot! I told you to keep her door locked!

NURSIE: She jimmied the lock, Esmeralda!

[*These shouts are mostly lost in the general rhubarb of the chase and the shouting Street People. Esmeralda crouches on the forestage, screaming encouragement in Spanish to the fugitive. Abdullah catches sight of her, seizes her wrist, shouting:*]

ABDULLAH: Here she is! I got her!

[*Esmeralda fights savagely. She nearly breaks loose, but Nursie and the Gypsy close upon her, too, and she is overwhelmed and dragged back, fighting all the way, toward the door from which she escaped. Meanwhile—timed with the above action—shots are fired in the air by Kilroy's pursuers. He dashes, panting, into the boxes of the theatre, darting from one box to another, shouting incoherently, now, sobbing for breath, crying out:*]

KILROY: Mary, help a Christian! Help a Christian, Mary!

ESMERALDA: Yankee! Yankee, jump!

[*The Officers close upon him in the box nearest the stage. A dazzling spot of light is thrown on him. He lifts a little gilded chair to defend himself. The chair is torn from his grasp. He leaps upon the ledge of the box.*]

Jump! Jump, Yankee!

[*The Gypsy is dragging the girl back by her hair.*]

KILROY: Watch out down there! Geronimo!

[*He leaps onto the stage and crumples up with a twisted ankle. Esmeralda screams demoniacally, breaks from her mother's grasp and rushes to him, fighting off his pursuers who have leapt after him from the box. Abdullah, Nursie and the Gypsy seize her again, just as Kilroy is seized by his pursuers. The Officers beat him to his knees. Each time he is struck, Esmeralda screams as if she received the blow herself. As his cries subside into sobbing, so do hers, and at the end, when he is quite helpless, she is also overcome by her captors and as they drag her back to the Gypsy's she cries to him:*]

ESMERALDA: They've got you! They've got me!

[*Her mother slaps her fiercely.*]

Caught! Caught! We're caught!

[*She is dragged inside. The door is slammed shut on her continuing outcries. For a moment nothing is heard but Kilroy's hoarse panting and sobbing. Gutman takes command of the situation, thrusting his way through the crowd to face Kilroy who is pinioned by two Guards.*]

GUTMAN [*smiling serenely*]: Well, well, how do you do! I understand that you're seeking employment here. We need a Patsy and the job is yours for the asking!

KILROY: I don't. Accept. This job. I been. Shanghied!

[*Kilroy dons Patsy outfit.*]

GUTMAN: Hush! The Patsy doesn't talk. He lights his nose, that's all!

GUARD: Press the little button at the end of the cord.

GUTMAN: That's right. Just press the little button at the end of the cord!

[*Kilroy lights his nose. Everybody laughs.*]

GUTMAN: Again, ha ha! Again, ha ha! Again!

[*The nose goes off and on like a firefly as the stage dims out.*]

THE CURTAIN FALLS. THERE IS A SHORT INTERMISSION.

The Dreamer is singing with mandolin, "Noche de Ronde." The Guests murmur, "Cool—cool . . ." Gutman stands on the podiumlike elevation downstage right, smoking a long thin cigar, signing an occasional tab from the bar or café. He is standing in an amber spot. The rest of the stage is filled with blue dusk. At the signal the song fades to a whisper and Gutman speaks.

GUTMAN: Block Seven on the Camino Real—

I like this hour.

[*He gives the audience a tender gold-toothed smile.*]

The fire's gone out of the day but the light of it lingers . . . In Rome the continual fountains are bathing stone heroes with silver, in Copenhagen the Tivoli Gardens are lighted, they're selling the lottery on San Juan de Latrene . . .

[*The Dreamer advances a little, playing the mandolin softly.*]

LA MADRECITA [*holding up glass beads and shell necklaces*]: Recuerdos, recuerdos?

GUTMAN: And these are the moments when we look into ourselves and ask with a wonder which never is lost altogether: "Can this be all? Is there nothing more? Is this what the glittering wheels of the heavens turn for?"

[*He leans forward as if conveying a secret.*]

—Ask the Gypsy! Un poco dinero will tickle the Gypsy's palm and give her visions!

[*Abdullah emerges with a silver tray, calling:*]

ABDULLAH: Letter for Signor Casanova, letter for Signor Casanova!

[*Jacques springs up but stands rigid.*]

GUTMAN: Casanova, you have received a letter. Perhaps it's the letter with the remittance check in it!

JACQUES [*in a hoarse, exalted voice*]: Yes! It is! The letter! With the remittance check in it!

GUTMAN: Then why don't you take it so you can maintain your residence at the Siete Mares and so avoid the more somber attractions of the "Ritz Men Only"?

JACQUES: My hand is—

GUTMAN: Your hand is paralyzed?. . . . By what? *Anxiety? Apprehension?* . . . Put the letter in Signor Casanova's pocket so he can open it when he recovers the use of his digital extremities. Then give him a shot of brandy on the house before he falls on his face!

[*Jacques has stepped down into the plaza. He looks down at Kilroy crouched to the right of him and wildly blinking his nose.*]

JACQUES: Yes. I know the Morse code.

[*Kilroy's nose again blinks on and off.*]

Thank you, brother.

[*This is said as if acknowledging a message.*]

I knew without asking the Gypsy that something of this sort would happen to you. You have a spark of anarchy in your spirit and that's not to be tolerated. Nothing wild or honest is tolerated here! It has to be extinguished or used only to light up your nose for Mr. Gutman's amusement . . .

[*Jacques saunters around Kilroy whistling "La Golondrina." Then satisfied that no one is suspicious of this encounter . . .*]

Before the final block we'll find some way out of here! Meanwhile, patience and courage, little brother!

[*Jacques feeling he's been there too long starts away giving Kilroy a reassuring pat on the shoulder and saying:*]

Patience! . . . Courage!

LADY MULLIGAN [*from the Mulligans' table*]: Mr. Gutman!

GUTMAN: Lady Mulligan! And how are you this evening, Lord Mulligan?

45

LADY MULLIGAN [*interrupting Lord Mulligan's rumblings*]: He's not at all well. This . . . climate is so enervating!

LORD MULLIGAN: I was so weak this morning . . . I couldn't screw the lid on my tooth paste!

LADY MULLIGAN: Raymond, tell Mr. Gutman about those two impertinent workmen in the square! . . . These two idiots pushing a white barrel! Pop up every time we step outside the hotel!

LORD MULLIGAN: —point and giggle at me!

LADY MULLIGAN: Can't they be discharged?

GUTMAN: They can't be discharged, disciplined nor bribed! All you can do is pretend to ignore them.

LADY MULLIGAN: I can't eat! . . . Raymond, stop stuffing!

LORD MULLIGAN: *Shut up!*

GUTMAN [*to the audience*]: When the big wheels crack on this street it's like the fall of a capital city, the destruction of Carthage, the sack of Rome by the white-eyed giants from the North! I've seen them fall! I've seen the destruction of them! Adventurers suddenly frightened of a dark room! Gamblers unable to choose between odd and even! Con men and pitchmen and plume-hatted cavaliers turned baby-soft at one note of the Streetcleaners' pipes! When I observe this change, I say to myself: "Could it happen to ME?"—The answer is "YES!" And that's what curdles my blood like milk on the doorstep of someone gone for the summer!

[*A Hunchback Mummer somersaults through his hoop of silver bells, springs up and shakes it excitedly toward a downstage arch which begins to flicker with a diamond-blue radiance; this marks the advent of each legendary character in the play. The music follows: a waltz from the time of Camille in Paris.*]

GUTMAN [*downstage to the audience*]: Ah, there's the music of another legend, one that everyone knows, the legend of the sentimental whore, the courtesan who made the mistake of love. But now you see her coming into this plaza not as she was when she burned with a fever that cast a thin light over Paris, but changed, yes, faded as lanterns and legends fade when they burn into day!

[*He turns and shouts:*]

Rosita, sell her a flower!

[*Marguerite has entered the plaza. A beautiful woman of indefinite age. The Street People cluster about her with wheedling cries, holding up glass beads, shell necklaces and so forth. She seems confused, lost, half-awake. Jacques has sprung up at her entrance but has difficulty making his way through the cluster of vendors. Rosita has snatched up a tray of flowers and cries out:*]

ROSITA: Camellias, camellias! Pink or white, whichever a lady finds suitable to the moon!

GUTMAN: That's the ticket!

MARGUERITE: Yes, I would like a camellia.

ROSITA [*in a bad French accent*]: Rouge ou blanc ce soir?

MARGUERITE: It's always a white one, now . . . but there used to be five evenings out of the month when a pink camellia, instead of the usual white one, let my admirers know that the moon those nights was unfavorable to pleasure, and so they called me—Camille . . .

JACQUES: Mia cara!

[*Imperiously, very proud to be with her, he pushes the Street People aside with his cane.*]

Out of the way, make way, let us through, please!

MARGUERITE: Don't push them with your cane.

JACQUES: If they get close enough they'll snatch your purse.

[*Marguerite utters a low, shocked cry.*]

What is it?

MARGUERITE: *My purse is gone! It's lost! My papers were in it!*

JACQUES: Your passport was in it?

MARGUERITE: My passport and my permiso de residencia!

[*She leans faint against the arch during the following scene. Abdullah turns to run. Jacques catches him.*]

JACQUES [*seizing Abdullah's wrist*]: Where did you take her?

ABDULLAH: Oww!—P'tit Zoco.

JACQUES: The Souks?

ABDULLAH: The Souks!

JACQUES: Which cafés did she go to?

ABDULLAH: Ahmed's, she went to—

JACQUES: Did she smoke at Ahmed's?

ABDULLAH: Two kif pipes!

JACQUES: Who was it took her purse? Was it *you*? We'll see!

[*He strips off the boy's burnoose. He crouches whimpering, shivering in a ragged slip.*]

MARGUERITE: Jacques, let the boy go, he didn't take it!

JACQUES: He doesn't have it on him but knows who does!

ABDULLAH: No, no, I don't know!

JACQUES: You little son of a Gypsy! Senta! . . . You know who I am? I am Jacques Casanova! I belong to the Secret Order of the Rose-colored Cross! . . . Run back to Ahmed's. Contact the spiv that took the lady's purse. Tell him to keep it but give her back her papers! There'll be a large reward.

[*He thumps his cane on the ground to release Abdullah from the spell. The boy dashes off. Jacques laughs and turns triumphantly to Marguerite.*]

LADY MULLIGAN: Waiter! That adventurer and his mistress must not be seated next to Lord Mulligan's table!

JACQUES [*loudly enough for Lady Mulligan to hear*]: This hotel has become a mecca for black marketeers and their expensively kept women!

LADY MULLIGAN: Mr. Gutman!

MARGUERITE: Let's have dinner upstairs!

WAITER [*directing them to terrace table*]: This way, M'sieur.

JACQUES: We'll take our usual table.

[*He indicates one.*]

MARGUERITE: Please!

WAITER [*overlapping Marguerite's "Please!"*]: This table is reserved for Lord Byron!

JACQUES [*masterfully*]: This table is always our table.

MARGUERITE: I'm not hungry.

JACQUES: Hold out the lady's chair, cretino!

GUTMAN [*darting over to Marguerite's chair*]: Permit me!

[*Jacques bows with mock gallantry to Lady Mulligan as he turns to his chair during seating of Marguerite.*]

LADY MULLIGAN: We'll move to *that* table!

JACQUES: —You must learn how to carry the banner of Bohemia into the enemy camp.

[*A screen is put up around them.*]

MARGUERITE: Bohemia has no banner. It survives by discretion.

JACQUES: I'm glad that you value discretion. *Wine list!* Was it discretion that led you through the bazaars this afternoon wearing your cabochon sapphire and diamond eardrops? You were fortunate that you lost only your purse and papers!

MARGUERITE: Take the wine list.

JACQUES: Still or sparkling?

MARGUERITE: Sparkling.

GUTMAN: May I make a suggestion, Signor Casanova?

JACQUES: Please do.

GUTMAN: It's a very cold and dry wine from only ten metres below the snowline in the mountains. The name of the wine is Quando!— meaning when! Such as "When are remittances going to be received?"

"When are accounts to be settled?" Ha ha ha! Bring Signor Casanova a bottle of Quando with the compliments of the house!

JACQUES: I'm sorry this had to happen in—your presence . . .

MARGUERITE: That doesn't matter, my dear. But why don't you *tell* me when you are short of money?

JACQUES: I thought the fact was apparent. It is to everyone else.

MARGUERITE: The letter you were expecting, it still hasn't come?

JACQUES [*removing it from his pocket*]: It came this afternoon— Here it is!

MARGUERITE: You haven't opened the letter!

JACQUES: I haven't had the nerve to! I've had so many unpleasant surprises that I've lost faith in my luck.

MARGUERITE: Give the letter to me. Let me open it for you.

JACQUES: Later, a little bit later, after the—wine . . .

MARGUERITE: Old hawk, anxious old hawk!

[*She clasps his hand on the table; he leans toward her; she kisses her fingertips and places them on his lips.*]

JACQUES: Do you call that a kiss?

MARGUERITE: I call it the ghost of a kiss. It will have to do for now.

[*She leans back, her blue-tinted eyelids closed.*]

JACQUES: Are you tired? Are you tired, Marguerite? You know you should have rested this afternoon.

MARGUERITE: I looked at silver and rested.

JACQUES: You looked at silver at Ahmed's?

MARGUERITE: No, I rested at Ahmed's, and had mint tea.

[*The Dreamer accompanies their speech with his guitar. The duo-logue should have the style of an antiphonal poem, the cues picked up so that there is scarcely a separation between the speeches, and the tempo quick and the voices edged.*]

JACQUES: You had mint tea downstairs?

MARGUERITE: No, upstairs.

JACQUES: Upstairs where they burn the poppy?

MARGUERITE: Upstairs where it's cool and there's music and the haggling of the bazaar is soft as the murmur of pigeons.

JACQUES: That sounds restful. Reclining among silk pillows on a divan, in a curtained and perfumed alcove above the bazaar?

MARGUERITE: Forgetting for a while where I am, or that I don't know where I am . . .

JACQUES: Forgetting alone or forgetting with some young companion who plays the lute or the flute or who had silver to show you? Yes. That sounds very restful. And yet you do seem tired.

MARGUERITE: If I seem tired, it's your insulting solicitude that I'm tired of!

JACQUES: Is it insulting to feel concern for your safety in this place?

MARGUERITE: Yes, it is. The implication is.

JACQUES: What is the implication?

MARGUERITE: You know what it is: that I am one of those *aging— voluptuaries*—who used to be paid for pleasure but now have to pay!—Jacques, I won't be followed, I've gone too far to be followed!— *What is it?*

[*The Waiter has presented an envelope on a salver.*]

WAITER: A letter for the lady.

MARGUERITE: How strange to receive a letter in a place where nobody knows I'm staying! Will you open it for me?

[*The Waiter withdraws. Jacques takes the letter and opens it.*

Well! What is it?

JACQUES: Nothing important. An illustrated brochure from some resort in the mountains.

MARGUERITE: What is it called?

JACQUES: Bide-a-While.

[*A chafing dish bursts into startling blue flame at the Mulligans'* *table. Lady Mulligan clasps her hands and exclaims with affected* *delight, the Waiter and Mr. Gutman laugh agreeably. Marguerite* *springs up and moves out upon the forestage. Jacques goes to* *her.*]

Do you know this resort in the mountains?

MARGUERITE: Yes. I stayed there once. It's one of those places with open sleeping verandahs, surrounded by snowy pine woods. It has rows and rows of narrow white iron beds as regular as tombstones. The invalids smile at each other when axes flash across valleys, ring, flash, ring again! Young voices shout across valleys Hola! And mail is delivered. The friend that used to write you ten-page letters contents himself now with a post card bluebird that tells you to "Get well quick!"

[*Jacques throws the brochure away.*]

—And when the last bleeding comes, not much later nor earlier than expected, you're wheeled discreetly into a little tent of white gauze, and the last thing you know of this world, of which you've known so little and yet so much, is the smell of an empty icebox.

[*The blue flame expires in the chafing dish. Gutman fields up the* *brochure and hands it to the Waiter, whispering something.*]

JACQUES: You won't go back to that place.

[*The Waiter places the brochure on the salver again and approaches* *behind them.*]

MARGUERITE: I wasn't released. I left without permission. They sent me this to remind me.

WAITER [*presenting the salver*]: You dropped this.

JACQUES: We threw it away!

WAITER: Excuse me.

JACQUES: Now, from now on, Marguerite, you must take better care of yourself. Do you hear me?

MARGUERITE: I hear you. No more distractions for me? No more entertainers in curtained and perfumed alcoves above the bazaar, no more young men that a pinch of white powder or a puff of gray smoke can almost turn to someone devoutly remembered?

JACQUES: No, from now on—

MARGUERITE: What "from now on," old hawk?

JACQUES: Rest. Peace.

MARGUERITE: Rest in peace is that final bit of advice they carve on gravestones, and I'm not ready for it! Are you? Are *you* ready for it?

[*She returns to the table. He follows her.*]

Oh, Jacques, when are we going to leave here, how are we going to leave here, you've got to tell me!

JACQUES: I've told you all I know.

MARGUERITE: Nothing, you've given up hope!

JACQUES: I haven't, that's not true.

[*Gutman has brought out the white cockatoo which he shows to Lady Mulligan at her table.*]

GUTMAN [*his voice rising above the murmurs*]: Her name is Aurora.

LADY MULLIGAN: Why do you call her Aurora?

GUTMAN: She cries at daybreak.

LADY MULLIGAN: Only at daybreak?

GUTMAN: Yes, at daybreak only.

[*Their voices and laughter fade under.*]

MARGUERITE: How long is it since you've been to the travel agencies?

JACQUES: This morning I made the usual round of Cook's, American Express, Wagon-lits Universal, and it was the same story. There are no flights out of here till further orders from someone higher up.

MARGUERITE: Nothing, nothing at all?

JACQUES: Oh, there's a rumor of something called the Fugitivo, but—

MARGUERITE: The What!!!?

JACQUES: The Fugitivo. It's one of those nonscheduled things that—

MARGUERITE: When, when, when?

JACQUES: I told you it was nonscheduled. Nonscheduled means it comes and goes at no predictable—

MARGUERITE: Don't give me the dictionary! I want to know how does one get on it? Did you bribe them? Did you offer them money? No. Of course you didn't! And I know why! You really don't want to leave here. You *think* you don't want to go because you're brave as an old hawk. But the truth of the matter—the real not the royal truth—is that you're terrified of the Terra Incognita outside that wall.

JACQUES: You've hit upon the truth. I'm terrified of the unknown country inside or outside this wall or any place on earth without you with me! The only country, known or unknown that I can breathe in, or care to, is the country in which we breathe together, as we are now at this table. And later, a little while later, even closer than this, the sole inhabitants of a tiny world whose limits are those of the light from a rose-colored lamp—beside the sweetly, completely known country of your cool bed!

MARGUERITE: The little comfort of love?

JACQUES: Is that comfort so little?

MARGUERITE: Caged birds accept each other but flight is what they long for.

JACQUES: I want to stay here with you and love you and guard you until the time or way comes that we both can leave with honor.

MARGUERITE: "Leave with honor"? Your vocabulary is almost as out-of-date as your cape and your cane. How could anyone quit this field with honor, this place where there's nothing but the gradual wasting away of everything decent in us . . . the sort of desperation that comes after even desperation has been worn out through long wear! . . . Why have they put these screens around the table?

[*She springs up and knocks one of them over.*]

LADY MULLIGAN: There! You see? I don't understand why you let such people stay here.

GUTMAN: They pay the price of admission the same as you.

LADY MULLIGAN: What price is that?

GUTMAN: Desperation!—With cash here!

[*He indicates the Siete Mares.*]

Without cash there!

[*He indicates Skid Row.*]

Block Eight on the Camino Real!

There is the sound of loud desert wind and a flamenco cry followed by a dramatic phrase of music.

A flickering diamond-blue radiance floods the hotel entrance. The crouching, grimacing Hunchback shakes his hoop of bells which is the convention for the appearance of each legendary figure.

Lord Byron appears in the doorway readied for departure. Gutman raises his hand for silence.

GUTMAN: You're leaving us, Lord Byron?

BYRON: Yes, I'm leaving you, Mr. Gutman.

GUTMAN: What a pity! But this is a port of entry and departure. There are no permanent guests. Possibly you are getting a little restless?

BYRON: The luxuries of this place have made me soft. The metal point's gone from my pen, there's nothing left but the feather.

GUTMAN: That may be true. But what can you do about it?

BYRON: Make a departure!

GUTMAN: From yourself?

BYRON: From my present self to myself as I used to be!

GUTMAN: *That's* the *furthest* departure a man could make! I guess you're sailing to Athens? There's another war there and like all wars since the beginning of time it can be interpreted as a—struggle for *what?*

BYRON: —For *freedom!* You may laugh at it, but it still means something to *me!*

GUTMAN: Of course it does! I'm not laughing a bit, I'm beaming with admiration.

BYRON: I've allowed myself many distractions.

GUTMAN: Yes, indeed!

BYRON: But I've never altogether forgotten my old devotion to the—

GUTMAN: —To the *what*, Lord Byron?

[*Byron passes nervous fingers through his hair.*]

You can't remember the object of your one-time devotion?

[*There is a pause. Byron limps away from the terrace and goes toward the fountain.*]

BYRON: When Shelley's corpse was recovered from the sea . . .

[*Gutman beckons the Dreamer who approaches and accompanies Byron's speech.*]

—It was burned on the beach at Viareggio.—I watched the spectacle from my carriage because the stench was revolting . . . Then it—fascinated me! I got out of my carriage. Went nearer, holding a handkerchief to my nostrils!—I saw that the front of the skull had broken away in the flames, and there—

[*He advances out upon the stage apron, followed by Abdullah with the pine torch or lantern.*]

And there was the brain of Shelley, indistinguishable from a cooking *stew!*—*boiling, bubbling, hissing!*—in the *blackening—cracked— pot*—of his skull!

[*Marguerite rises abruptly. Jacques supports her.*]

—Trelawney, his friend, Trelawney, threw salt and oil and frankincense in the flames and finally the almost intolerable stench—

[*Abdullah giggles. Gutman slaps him.*]

—was *gone* and the burning was *pure!*—as a man's burning should be . . . A man's burning *ought* to be pure!—*not* like mine—(a crepe suzette—burned in brandy . . .) *Shelley's* burning was finally very *pure!* But the body, the corpse, split open like a grilled pig!

[*Abdullah giggles irrepressibly again. Gutman grips the back of his neck and he stands up stiff and assumes an expression of exaggerated solemnity.*]

—And then Trelawney—as the ribs of the corpse unlocked—reached into them as a baker reaches quickly into an oven!

[*Abdullah almost goes into another convulsion.*]

—And snatched out—as a baker would a biscuit!—the *heart* of Shelley! Snatched the heart of Shelley out of the blistering corpse!—Out of the purifying—blue flame . . .

[*Marguerite resumes her seat; Jacques his.*]

—And it was *over!*—I thought—

[*He turns slightly from the audience and crosses upstage from the apron. He faces Jacques and Marguerite.*]

—I thought it was a disgusting thing to do, to snatch a man's heart from his body! What can one man do with another man's heart?

[*Jacques rises and strides the stage with his cane.*]

JACQUES [*passionately*]: He can do this with it!

[*He seizes a loaf of bread on his table, and descends from the terrace.*]

He can twist it like this!

[*He twists the loaf.*]

He can tear it like this!

[*He tears the loaf in two.*]

He can crush it under his foot!

[*He drops the bread and stamps on it.*]

—*And kick it away—like this!*

[*He kicks the bread off the terrace. Lord Byron turns away from him and limps again out upon the stage apron and speaks to the audience.*]

BYRON: That's very true, Señor. But a poet's vocation, which used to be my vocation, is to influence the heart in a gentler fashion than you have made your mark on that loaf of bread. He ought to purify it and lift it above its ordinary level. For what is the heart but a sort of—

[*He makes a high, groping gesture in the air.*]

—A sort of—*instrument*—that translates *noise* into *music,* chaos into—*order* . . .

[*Abdullah ducks almost to the earth in an effort to stifle his mirth. Gutman coughs to cover his own amusement.*]

—a *mysterious order!*

[*He raises his voice till it fills the plaza.*]

—That was my vocation once upon a time, before it was obscured by vulgar plaudits!—Little by little it was lost among gondolas and palazzos!—masked balls, glittering salons, huge shadowy courts and torch-lit entrances!—Baroque façades, canopies and carpets, candelabra and gold plate among snowy damask, ladies with throats as slender as flower stems, bending and breathing toward me their fragrant breath—

—Exposing their breasts to me!

Whispering, half smiling!—And everywhere marble, the visible grandeur of marble, pink and gray marble, veined and tinted as flayed corrupting flesh,—all these provided agreeable distractions from the rather frightening solitude of a poet. Oh, I wrote many cantos in Venice and Constantinople and in Ravenna and Rome, on all of those Latin and Levantine excursions that my twisted foot led me into—but I wonder about them a little. They seem to improve as the wine in the bottle—dwindles . . . *There is a passion for declivity in this world!*

And lately I've found myself listening to hired musicians behind a row of artificial palm trees—instead of the single—pure-stringed instrument of my heart . . .

Well, then, it's time to leave here! [*He turns back to the stage.*]

—There is a time for departure even when there's no certain place to go!

I'm going to look for one, now. I'm sailing to Athens. At least I can look up at the Acropolis, I can stand at the foot of it and look up at broken columns on the crest of a hill—if not purity, at least its recollection . . .

I can sit quietly looking for a long, long time in absolute silence, and possibly, yes, *still* possibly—

The old pure music will come to me again. Of course on the other hand I may hear only the little noise of insects in the grass . . .

But I am sailing to Athens! *Make voyages!—Attempt them!*—there's nothing else . . .

MARGUERITE [*excitedly*]: Watch where he goes!

[*Lord Byron limps across the plaza with his head bowed, making slight, apologetic gestures to the wheedling Beggars who shuffle about him. There is music. He crosses toward the steep Alleyway Out. The following is played with a quiet intensity so it will be in a lower key than the later Fugitivo Scene.*]

Watch him, watch him, see which way he goes. Maybe he knows of a way that we haven't found out.

JACQUES: Yes, I'm watching him, cara.

[*Lord and Lady Mulligan half rise, staring anxiously through monocle and lorgnon.*]

MARGUERITE: Oh, my God, I believe he's going up that alley.

JACQUES: Yes, he is. He has.

LORD and LADY MULLIGAN: Oh, the fool, the idiot, he's going under the arch!

MARGUERITE: Jacques, run after him, warn him, tell him about the desert he has to cross.

JACQUES: I think he knows what he's doing.

MARGUERITE: I can't look!

[*She turns to the audience, throwing back her head and closing her eyes. The desert wind sings loudly as Byron climbs to the top of the steps.*]

BYRON [*to several porters carrying luggage—which is mainly caged birds*]: THIS WAY!

[*He exits. Kilroy starts to follow. He stops at the steps, cringing and looking at Gutman. Gutman motions him to go ahead. Kilroy rushes up the stairs. He looks out, loses his nerve and sits—blinking his nose. Gutman laughs as he announces—*]

GUTMAN: Block Nine on the Camino Real!

[*He goes into the hotel.*]

Abdullah runs back to the hotel with the billowing flambeau. A faint and faraway humming sound becomes audible . . . Marguerite opens her eyes with a startled look. She searches the sky for something. A very low percussion begins with the humming sound, as if excited hearts are beating.

MARGUERITE: Jacques! I hear something in the sky!

JACQUES: I think what you hear is—

MARGUERITE [*with rising excitement*]: —No, it's a plane, a great one, I see the lights of it, now!

JACQUES: Some kind of fireworks, cara.

MARGUERITE: Hush! LISTEN!

[*She blows out the candle to see better above it. She rises, peering into the sky.*]

I see it! I see it! There! It's circling over us!

LADY MULLIGAN: Raymond, Raymond, sit down, your face is flushed!

HOTEL GUESTS [*overlapping*]: —What is it?

—The FUGITIVO!

—THE FUGITIVO! THE FUGITIVO!

—Quick, get my jewelry from the hotel safe!

—Cash a check!

—Throw some things in a bag! I'll wait here!

—Never mind luggage, we have our money and papers!

—Where is it now?

—There, there!

—It's turning to land!

—To go like this?

—Yes, go anyhow, just go anyhow, just go!

—Raymond! Please!

—Oh, it's rising again!

—Oh, it's—*SHH! MR. GUTMAN!*

[*Gutman appears in the doorway. He raises a hand in a commanding gesture.*]

GUTMAN: Signs in the sky should not be mistaken for wonders!

[*The Voices modulate quickly.*]

Ladies, gentlemen, please resume your seats!

[*Places are resumed at tables, and silver is shakily lifted. Glasses are raised to lips, but the noise of concerted panting of excitement fills the stage and a low percussion echoes frantic heart beats. Gutman descends to the plaza, shouting furiously to the Officer.*]

Why wasn't I told the Fugitivo was coming?

[*Everyone, almost as a man, rushes into the hotel and reappears almost at once with hastily collected possessions. Marguerite rises but appears stunned. There is a great whistling and screeching sound as the aerial transport halts somewhere close by, accompanied by rainbow splashes of light and cries like children's on a roller coaster. Some incoming Passengers approach the stage down an aisle of the theatre, preceded by Redcaps with luggage.*]

PASSENGERS: —What a heavenly trip!

—The scenery was thrilling!

—It's so quick!

—The only way to travel! Etc., etc.

[*A uniformed man, the Pilot, enters the plaza with a megaphone.*]

PILOT [*through the megaphone*]: Fugitivo now loading for departure! Fugitivo loading immediately for departure! Northwest corner of the plaza!

MARGUERITE: Jacques, it's the Fugitivo, it's the nonscheduled thing you heard of this afternoon!

PILOT: All out-going passengers on the Fugitivo are requested to present their tickets and papers immediately at this station.

MARGUERITE: He said "outgoing passengers"!

PILOT: Outgoing passengers on the Fugitivo report immediately at this station for customs inspection.

MARGUERITE [*with a forced smile*]: Why are you just standing there?

JACQUES [*with an Italian gesture*]: Che cosa possa fare!

MARGUERITE: Move, move, do something!

JACQUES: *What!*

MARGUERITE: Go to them, ask, find out!

JACQUES: I have no idea what the damned thing is!

MARGUERITE: I do, I'll tell you! It's a way to escape from this abominable place!

JACQUES: Forse, forse, non so!

MARGUERITE: It's a way *out* and *I'm* not going to miss it!

PILOT: Ici la Douane! Customs inspection here!

MARGUERITE: Customs. That means luggage. Run to my room! Here! Key! Throw a few things in a bag, my jewels, my furs, but hurry! Vite, vite, vite! I don't believe there's much time! No, everybody is—

[*Outgoing Passengers storm the desk and table.*]

—Clamoring for tickets! There must be limited space! Why don't you do what I tell you?

[*She rushes to a man with a rubber stamp and a roll of tickets.*]

Monsieur! Señor! Pardonnez-moi! I'm going, I'm going out! I want my ticket!

PILOT [*coldly*]: Name, please.

MARGUERITE: Mademoiselle—Gautier—but I—

PILOT: Gautier? Gautier? We have no Gautier listed.

MARGUERITE: I'm—*not* listed! I mean I'm—traveling under another name.

TRAVEL AGENT: What name are you traveling under?

[*Prudence and Olympe rush out of the hotel half dressed, dragging their furs. Meanwhile Kilroy is trying to make a fast buck or two as a Redcap. The scene gathers wild momentum, is punctuated by crashes of percussion. Grotesque mummers act as demon custom inspectors and immigration authorities, etc. Baggage is tossed about, ripped open, smuggled goods seized, arrests made, all amid the wildest importunities, protests, threats, bribes, entreaties; it is a scene for improvisation.*]

PRUDENCE: Thank God I woke up!

OLYMPE: Thank God I wasn't asleep!

PRUDENCE: I knew it was nonscheduled but I *did* think they'd give you time to get in your girdle.

OLYMPE: Look who's trying to crash it! I know damned well *she* don't have a reservation!

PILOT [*to Marguerite*]: What name did you say, Mademoiselle? Please! People are waiting, you're holding up the line!

MARGUERITE: I'm so confused! Jacques! What name did you make my reservation under?

OLYMPE: She has no reservation!

PRUDENCE: *I have, I got mine!*

OLYMPE: *I got mine!*

PRUDENCE: *I'm* next!

OLYMPE: Don't push *me*, you old bag!

MARGUERITE: I was here first! I was here before anybody! Jacques, quick! Get my money from the hotel safe!

[*Jacques exits.*]

AGENT: *Stay in line!*

[*There is a loud warning whistle.*]

PILOT: Five minutes. The Fugitivo leaves in five minutes. Five, five minutes only!

[*At this announcement the scene becomes riotous.*]

TRAVEL AGENT: *Four minutes! The Fugitivo leaves in four minutes!*

[*Prudence and Olympe are shrieking at him in French. The warning whistle blasts again.*]

Three minutes, the Fugitivo leaves in three minutes!

MARGUERITE [*topping the turmoil*]: Monsieur! Please! I was here first, I was here before anybody! Look!

[*Jacques returns with her money.*]

I have thousands of francs! Take whatever you want! Take all of it, it's yours!

PILOT: Payment is only accepted in pounds sterling or dollars. Next, please.

MARGUERITE: You don't accept francs? They do at the hotel! They accept my francs at the Siete Mares!

PILOT: Lady, don't argue with me, I don't make the rules!

MARGUERITE [*beating her forehead with her fist*]: Oh, God, Jacques! Take these back to the cashier!

[*She thrusts the bills at him.*]

Get them changed to dollars or—*Hurry! Tout de suite!* I'm—going to faint . . .

JACQUES: But Marguerite—

MARGUERITE: *Go! Go! Please!*

PILOT: Closing, we're closing now! The Fugitivo leaves in two minutes!

[*Lord and Lady Mulligan rush forward.*]

LADY MULLIGAN: Let Lord Mulligan through.

PILOT [*to Marguerite*]: You're standing in the way.

[*Olympe screams as the Customs Inspector dumps her jewels on the ground. She and Prudence butt heads as they dive for the gems: the fight is renewed.*]

MARGUERITE [*detaining the Pilot*]: Oh, look, Monsieur! Regardez ça! My diamond, a solitaire-two carats! Take that as security!

PILOT: Let me go. The Loan Shark's across the plaza!

[*There is another warning blast. Prudence and Olympe seize hat boxes and rush toward the whistle.*]

MARGUERITE [*clinging desperately to the Pilot*]: You don't understand! Señor Casanova has gone to change money! He'll be here in a second. And I'll pay five, ten, twenty times the price of—*JACQUES! JACQUES! WHERE ARE YOU?*

VOICE [*back of auditorium*]: We're closing the gate!

MARGUERITE: You can't close the gate!

PILOT: Move, Madame!

MARGUERITE: I won't move!

LADY MULLIGAN: I tell you, Lord Mulligan is the Iron & Steel man from Cobh! Raymond! They're closing the gate!

LORD MULLIGAN: I can't seem to get through!

GUTMAN: Hold the gate for Lord Mulligan!

PILOT [*to Marguerite*]: Madame, stand back or I will have to use force!

MARGUERITE: Jacques! Jacques!

LADY MULLIGAN: Let us through! We're clear!

PILOT: Madame! Stand back and let these passengers through!

MARGUERITE: No, No! I'm first! I'm next!

LORD MULLIGAN: Get her out of our way! That woman's a whore!

LADY MULLIGAN: How dare you stand in our way?

PILOT: Officer, take this woman!

LADY MULLIGAN: Come on, Raymond!

MARGUERITE [*as the Officer pulls her away*]: Jacques! Jacques! Jacques!

[*Jacques returns with changed money.*]

Here! Here is the money!

PILOT: All right, give me your papers.

MARGUERITE: —My papers? Did you say my papers?

PILOT: Hurry, hurry, your passport!

MARGUERITE: —Jacques! He wants my papers! Give him my papers, Jacques!

JACQUES: —The lady's papers are lost!

MARGUERITE: [*wildly*]: No, no, no, THAT IS NOT TRUE! HE WANTS TO KEEP ME HERE! HE'S LYING ABOUT IT!

JACQUES: Have you forgotten that your papers were stolen?

MARGUERITE: I gave you my papers, I gave you my papers to keep, you've got my papers.

[*Screaming, Lady Mulligan breaks past her and descends the stairs.*]

LADY MULLIGAN: Raymond! Hurry!

LORD MULLIGAN [*staggering on the top step*]: I'm sick! I'm sick!

[*The Streetcleaners disguised as expensive morticians in swallow-tail coats come rapidly up the aisle of the theatre and wait at the foot of the stairway for the tottering tycoon.*]

LADY MULLIGAN: You cannot be sick till we get on the Fugitivo!

LORD MULLIGAN: Forward all cables to Guaranty Trust in Paris.

LADY MULLIGAN: Place de la Concorde.

LORD MULLIGAN: Thank you! All purchases C.O.D. to Mulligan Iron & Steel Works in Cobh—Thank you!

LADY MULLIGAN: Raymond! Raymond! Who are these men?

LORD MULLIGAN: I know these men! I recognize their faces!

LADY MULLIGAN: Raymond! They're the Streetcleaners!

[*She screams and runs up the aisle screaming repeatedly, stopping halfway to look back. The Two Streetcleaners seize Lord Mulligan by either arm as he crumples.*]

Pack Lord Mulligan's body in dry ice! Ship Air Express to Cobh care of Mulligan Iron & Steel Works, in Cobh!

[*She runs sobbing out of the back of the auditorium as the whistle blows repeatedly and a Voice shouts.*]

I'm coming! I'm coming!

MARGUERITE: Jacques! Jacques! Oh, God!

PILOT: The Fugitivo is leaving, all aboard!

[*He starts toward the steps. Marguerite clutches his arm.*]

Let go of me!

MARGUERITE: You can't go without me!

PILOT: Officer, hold this woman!

JACQUES: Marguerite, let him go!

[*She releases the Pilot's arm and turns savagely on Jacques. She tears his coat open, seizes a large envelope of papers and rushes after the Pilot who has started down the steps over the orchestra pit and into a center aisle of the house. Timpani build up as she starts down the steps, screaming—*]

MARGUERITE: Here! I have them here! Wait! I have my papers now, I have my papers!

[*The Pilot runs cursing up the center aisle as the Fugitivo whistle gives repeated short, shrill blasts; timpani and dissonant brass are heard.*

[*Outgoing Passengers burst into hysterical song, laughter, shouts of farewell. These can come over a loudspeaker at the back of the house.*]

VOICE IN DISTANCE: Going! Going! Going!

MARGUERITE [*attempting as if half paralyzed to descend the steps*]: NOT WITHOUT ME, NO, NO, NOT WITHOUT ME!

[*Her figure is caught in the dazzling glacial light of the follow-spot. It blinds her. She makes violent, crazed gestures, clinging to the railing of the steps; her breath is loud and hoarse as a dying persons, she holds a bloodstained handkerchief to her lips. There is a prolonged, gradually fading, rocketlike roar as the Fugitivo takes off. Shrill cries of joy from departing passengers; something radiant passes above the stage and streams of confetti and tinsel fall into the plaza. Then there is a great calm, the ship's receding roar diminished to the hum of an insect.*]

GUTMAN [*somewhat compassionately*]: Block Ten on the Camino Real.

There is something about the desolation of the plaza that suggests a city devastated by bombardment. Reddish lights flicker here and there as if ruins were smoldering and wisps of smoke rise from them.

LA MADRECITA [*almost inaudibly*]: Donde?

THE DREAMER: Aquí. Aquí, Madrecita.

MARGUERITE: Lost! Lost! Lost! Lost!

[*She is still clinging brokenly to the railing of the steps. Jacques descends to her and helps her back up the steps.*]

JACQUES: Lean against me, cara. Breathe quietly, now.

MARGUERITE: Lost!

JACQUES: Breathe quietly, quietly, and look up at the sky.

MARGUERITE: Lost . . .

JACQUES: These tropical nights are so clear. There's the Southern Cross. Do you see the Southern Cross, Marguerite?

[*He points through the proscenium. They are now on the bench before the fountain; she is resting in his arms.*]

And there, over there, is Orion, like a fat, golden fish swimming north in the deep clear water, and we are together, breathing quietly together, leaning together, quietly, quietly together, completely, sweetly together, not frightened, now, not alone, but completely quietly together . . .

[*La Madrecita, led into the center of the plaza by her son, has begun to sing very softly; the reddish flares dim out and the smoke disappears.*]

All of us have a desperate bird in our hearts, a memory of—some distant mother with—wings . . .

MARGUERITE: I would have—left—without you . . .

JACQUES: I know, I know!

MARGUERITE: Then how can you—still—?

JACQUES: Hold you?

[*Marguerite nods slightly.*]

Because you've taught me that part of love which is tender. I never knew it before. Oh, I had—mistresses that circled me like moons! I scrambled from one bed chamber to another bed chamber with shirt-tails always aflame, from girl to girl, like buckets of coal oil poured on a conflagration! But never loved until now with the part of love that's tender . . .

MARGUERITE: —We're used to each other. That's what you think is love . . . You'd better leave me now, you'd better go and let me go because there's a cold wind blowing out of the mountains and over the desert and into my heart, and if you stay with me now, I'll say cruel things, I'll wound your vanity, I'll taunt you with the decline of your male vigor!

JACQUES: Why does disappointment make people unkind to each other?

MARGUERITE: Each of us is very much alone.

JACQUES: Only if we distrust each other.

MARGUERITE: We have to distrust each other. It is our only defense against betrayal.

JACQUES: I think our defense is love.

MARGUERITE: Oh, Jacques, we're used to each other, we're a pair of captive hawks caught in the same cage, and so we've grown used to each other. That's what passes for love at this dim, shadowy end of the Camino Real . . .

What are we sure of? Not even of our existence, dear comforting friend! And whom can we ask the questions that torment us? "What is this place?" "Where are we?"—a fat old man who gives sly hints that only bewilder us more, a fake of a Gypsy squinting at cards and tea leaves. What else are we offered? The never-broken procession of little events that assure us that we and strangers about us are still going on! Where? Why? and the perch that we hold is unstable! We're threatened with eviction, for this is a port of entry and departure, there are no permanent guests! And where else have we to go when we leave here? Bide-a-While? "Ritz Men Only"? Or under that ominous arch into Terra Incognita? We're lonely. We're frightened. We hear the Streetcleaners' piping not far away. So now and then, although we've wounded each other time and again—we stretch out hands to each other in the dark that we can't escape from—we huddle together for some dim communal comfort—and that's what passes for love on this terminal stretch of the road that used to be royal. What is it, this feeling between us? When you feel my exhausted weight against your shoulder—when I clasp your anxious old hawk's head to my breast, what is it we feel in whatever is left of our hearts? Something, yes, something—delicate, unreal, bloodless! The sort of violets that could grow on the moon, or in the crevices of those far away mountains, fertilized by the droppings of carrion birds. Those birds are familiar to us. Their shadows inhabit the plaza. I've heard them flapping their wings like old charwomen beating worn-out carpets with gray brooms . . .

But tenderness, the violets in the mountains—can't break the rocks!

JACQUES: The violets in the mountains can break the rocks if you believe in them and allow them to grow!

[*The plaza has resumed its usual aspect. Abdullah enters through one of the downstage arches.*]

ABDULLAH: Get your carnival hats and noisemakers here! Tonight the moon will restore the virginity of my sister!

MARGUERITE [*almost tenderly touching his face*]: Don't you know that tonight I am going to betray you?

JACQUES: —Why would you do that?

MARGUERITE: Because I've outlived the tenderness of my heart. Abdullah, come here! I have an errand for you! Go to Ahmed's and deliver a message!

ABDULLAH: I'm working for Mama, making the Yankee dollar! Get your carnival hats and—

MARGUERITE: *Here, boy!*

73

[*She snatches a ring off her finger and offers it to him.*]

JACQUES: —Your cabochon sapphire?

MARGUERITE: Yes, my cabochon sapphire!

JACQUES: Are you mad?

MARGUERITE: Yes, I'm mad, or nearly! The specter of lunacy's at my heels tonight!

[*Jacques drives Abdullah back with his cane.*]

Catch, boy! The other side of the fountain! Quick!

[*The guitar is heard molto vivace. She tosses the ring across the fountain. Jacques attempts to hold the boy back with his cane. Abdullah dodges in and out like a little terrier, laughing. Marguerite shouts encouragement in French. When the boy is driven back from the ring, she snatches it up and tosses it to him again, shouting:*]

Catch, boy! Run to Ahmed's! Tell the charming young man that the French lady's bored with her company tonight! Say that the French lady missed the Fugitivo and wants to forget she missed it! Oh, and reserve a room with a balcony so I can watch your sister appear on the roof when the moonrise makes her a virgin!

[*Abdullah skips shouting out of the plaza. Jacques strides the stage with his cane. She says, without looking at him:*]

Time betrays us and we betray each other.

JACQUES: Wait, Marguerite.

MARGUERITE: No! I can't! The wind from the desert is sweeping me away!

[*A loud singing wind sweeps her toward the terrace, away from him. She looks back once or twice as if for some gesture of leave-taking but he only stares at her fiercely, striking the stage at intervals with his cane, like a death march. Gutman watches, smiling, from the terrace, bows to Marguerite as she passes into the hotel. The drum of Jacques' cane is taken up by other percussive instruments, and almost unnoticeably at first, weird-looking celebrants*] or *carnival mummers creep into the plaza, silently as spiders descending a wall.*

[*A sheet of scarlet and yellow rice paper bearing some cryptic device is lowered from the center of the plaza. The percussive effects become gradually louder. Jacques is oblivious to the scene behind him, standing in front of the plaza, his eyes closed.*]

GUTMAN: Block Eleven on the Camino Real.

GUTMAN: The Fiesta has started. The first event is the coronation of the King of Cuckolds.

[*Blinding shafts of light are suddenly cast upon Casanova on the forestage. He shields his face, startled, as the crowd closes about him. The blinding shafts of light seem to stride him like savage blows and he falls to his knees as—*

[*The Hunchback scuttles out of the Gypsy's stall with a crown of gilded antlers on a velvet pillow. He places it on Jacques' head. The celebrants form a circle about him chanting.*]

JACQUES: What is this?—a crown—

GUTMAN: A crown of horns!

CROWD: Cornudo! Cornudo! Cornudo! Cornudo! Cornudo!

GUTMAN: Hail, all hail, the King of Cuckolds on the Camino Real!

[*Jacques springs up, first striking out at them with his cane. Then all at once he abandons self-defense, throws off his cape, casts away his cane, and fills the plaza with a roar of defiance and self-derision.*]

JACQUES: Si, si, sono cornudo! Cornudo! Cornudo! Casanova is the King of Cuckolds on the Camino Real! Show me crowned to the world! Announce the honor! Tell the world of the honor bestowed on Casanova, Chevalier de Seingalt! Knight of the Golden Spur by the Grace of His Holiness the Pope . . . Famous adventurer! Con man Extraordinary! Gambler! Pitchman par excellence! Shill! Pimp! Spiv! And—great—lover . . .

[*The Crowd howls with applause and laughter but his voice rises above them with sobbing intensity.*]

Yes, I said GREAT LOVER! The greatest lover wears the longest horns on the Camino! GREAT! LOVER!

GUTMAN: Attention! Silence! The moon is rising! The restoration is about to occur!

[*A white radiance is appearing over the ancient wall of the town. The mountains become luminous. There is music. Everyone, with breathless attention, faces the light. Kilroy crosses to Jacques and beckons him out behind the crowd. There he snatches off the antlers and returns him his fedora. Jacques reciprocates by removing Kilroy's fright wig and electric nose. They embrace as brothers. In a Chaplinesque dumb-play, Kilroy points to the wildly flickering three brass balls of the Loan Shark and to his golden gloves: then with a terrible grimace he removes the gloves from about his neck, smiles at Jacques and indicates that the two of them together will take flight over the wall. Jacques shades his head sadly, pointing to his heart and then to the Siete Mares. Kilroy nods with regretful understanding of a human and manly folly. A Guard has been silently approaching them in a soft-shoe dance. Jacques whistles "La Golondrina." Kilroy assumes a very nonchalant pose. The Guard picks up curiously the discarded fright wig and electric nose. Then glancing suspiciously at the pair, he advances. Kilroy makes a run for it. He does a baseball slide into the Loan Shark's welcoming doorway. The door slams. The Cop is about to crash it when a gong sounds and Gutman shouts:*]

GUTMAN: SILENCE! ATTENTION! THE GYPSY!

GYPSY [*appearing on the roof with a gong*]: The moon has restored the virginity of my daughter Esmeralda!

[*The gong sounds.*]

STREET PEOPLE: Ahh!

GYPSY: The moon in its plenitude has made her a virgin!

[*The gong sounds.*]

STREET PEOPLE: Ahh!

GYPSY: Praise her, celebrate her, give her suitable homage!

[*The gong sounds.*]

STREET PEOPLE: Ahh!

GYPSY: Summon her to the roof! [*She shouts.*] ESMERALDA!

[*Dancers shout the name in rhythm.*]

RISE WITH THE MOON, MY DAUGHTER! CHOOSE THE HERO!

[*Esmeralda appears on the roof in dazzling light. She seems to be dressed in jewels. She raises her jeweled arms with a harsh flamenco cry.*]

ESMERALDA: OLE!

DANCERS: OLE!

[*The details of the Carnival are a problem for director and choreographer but it has already been indicated in the script that the Fiesta is a sort of serio-comic, grotesque-lyric "Rites of Fertility" with roots in various pagan cultures. It should not be overelaborated or allowed to occupy much time. It should not be more than three minutes from the appearance of Esmeralda on the Gypsy's roof till the return of Kilroy from the Loan Shark's. Kilroy emerges from the pawn shop in grotesque disguise, a turban, dark glasses, a burnoose and an umbrella or sunshade.*]

KILROY [*to Jacques*]: So long, pal, I wish you could come with me.

[*Jacques clasps his cross in Kilroy's hands.*]

ESMERALDA: Yankee!

KILROY [*to the audience*]: So long, everybody. Good luck to you all on the Camino! I hocked my golden gloves to finance this expedition. I'm going. Hasta luega. I'm going. I'm gone!

ESMERALDA: Yankee!

[*He has no sooner entered the plaza than the riotous women strip off everything but the dungarees and skivvy which he first appeared in.*]

KELROY [*to the women*]: Let me go. Let go of me! Watch out for my equipment!

ESMERALDA: Yankee! Yankee!

[*He breaks away from them and plunges up the stairs of the ancient wall. He is halfway up them when Gutman shouts out:*]

GUTMAN: Follow-spot on that gringo, light the stairs!

[*The light catches Kilroy. At the same instant Esmeralda cries out to him:*]

ESMERALDA: *Yankee! Yankee!*

GYPSY: What's goin' on down there?

[*She rushes into the plaza.*]

KILROY: Oh, no, I'm on my way out!

ESMERALDA: Espere un momento!

[*The Gypsy calls the police, but is ignored in the crowd.*]

KILROY: Don't tempt me, baby! I hocked my golden gloves to finance this expedition!

ESMERALDA: Querido!

KILROY: Querido means sweetheart, a word which is hard to resist but I must resist it.

ESMERALDA: Champ!

KILROY: I used to be Champ but why remind me of it?

ESMERALDA: Be Champ again! Contend in the contest! Compete in the competition!

GYPSY [*shouting*]: *Naw, naw, not eligible!*

ESMERALDA: *Pl-eeeeeeze!*

GYPSY: Slap her, Nursie, she's flippin'.

[*Esmeralda slaps Nursie instead.*]

ESMERALDA: Hero! Champ!

KILROY: I'm not in condition!

ESMERALDA: You're still the Champ, the undefeated Champ of the golden gloves!

KILROY: Nobody's called me that in a long, long time!

ESMERALDA: Champ!

KILROY: My resistance is crumbling!

ESMERALDA: Champ!

KILROY: It's crumbled!

ESMERALDA: Hero!

KILROY: GERONIMO!

[*He takes a flying leap from the stairs into the center of the plaza. He turns toward Esmeralda and cries:*]

DOLL!!

[*Kilroy surrounded by cheering Street People goes into a triumphant eccentric dance which reviews his history as fighter, traveler and lover. At finish of the dance, the music is cut off, as Kilroy lunges, arm uplifted toward Esmeralda, and cries:*]

KILROY: *Kilroy the Champ!*

ESMERALDA: *KILROY the Champ!*

[*She snatches a bunch of red roses from the stunned Nursie and tosses them to Kilroy.*]

CROWD [*sharply*]: OLE!

[*The Gypsy, at the same instant, hurls her gong down, creating a resounding noise. Kilroy turns and comes down toward the audience, saying to them:*]

KILROY: *Y'see?*

[*Cheering Street People surge toward him and lift him in the air. The lights fade as the curtain descends.*]

CROWD [*in a sustained yell*]: OLE!

THE CURTAIN FALLS. THERE IS A SHORT INTERMISSION.

The stage is in darkness except for a spotlight which picks out Esmeralda on the Gypsy's roof.

ESMERALDA: Mama, what happened? —Mama, the lights went out!— Mama, where are you? It's so dark I'm scared!—MAMA!

[*The lights are turned on displaying a deserted plaza. The Gypsy is seated at a small table before her stall.*]

GYPSY: Come on downstairs, Doll. The mischief is done. You've chosen your hero!

GUTMAN [*from the balcony of the Siete Mares*]: Block Twelve on the Camino Real.

NURSIE [*at the fountain*]: Gypsy, the fountain is still dry!

GYPSY: What d'yuh expect? There's nobody left to uphold the old traditions! You raise a girl. She watches television. Plays bebop. Reads *Screen Secrets*. Comes the Big Fiesta. The moonrise makes her a virgin—which is the neatest trick of the week! And what does she do? Chooses a Fugitive Patsy for the Chosen Hero! Well, show him in! Admit the joker and get the virgin ready!

NURSIE: You're going through with it?

GYPSY: Look, Nursie! I'm operating a legitimate joint! This joker'll get the same treatment he'd get if he breezed down the Camino in a blizzard of G-notes! Trot, girl! Lubricate your means of locomotion!

[*Nursie goes into the Gypsy's stall. The Gypsy rubs her hands together and blows on the crystal ball, spits on it and gives it the old one-two with a "shammy" rag . . . She mutters "Crystal ball, tell me all . . . crystal ball tell me all" . . . as: Kilroy bounds into the plaza from her stall . . . a rose between his teeth.*]

GYPSY: Siente se, por favor.

KILROY: No comprendo the lingo.

GYPSY: Put it down!

NURSIE [*offstage*]: Hey, Gypsy!

GYPSY: Address me as Madam!

NURSIE [*entering*]: *Madam!* Winchell has scooped you!

GYPSY: In a pig's eye!

NURSIE: The Fugitivo has *"fftt . . ."*!

GYPSY: In Elizabeth, New Jersey . . . ten fifty seven P.M . . . Eastern Standard Time—while you were putting them kiss-me-quicks in your hair-do! Furthermore, my second exclusive is that the solar system is drifting toward the constellation of Hercules: *Skiddoo!*

[*Nursie exits. Stamping is heard offstage.*]

Quiet, back there! God damn it!

NURSIE [*offstage*]: She's out of control!

GYPSY: Give her a double-bromide!

[*To Kilroy:*]

Well, how does it feel to be the Chosen Hero?

KILROY: I better explain something to you.

GYPSY: Save your breath. You'll need it.

KILROY: I want to level with you. Can I level with you?

GYPSY [*rapidly stamping some papers*]: How could you help but level with the Gypsy?

KILROY: I don't know what the hero is chosen for.

[*Esmeralda and Nursie shriek offstage.*]

GYPSY: Time will brief you . . . Aw, I hate paper work! . . . NURSEHH!

[*Nursie comes out and stands by the table.*]

This filing system is screwed up six ways from next Sunday . . . File this crap under crap!—

[*To Kilroy:*]

The smoking lamp is lit. Have a stick on me! [*She offers him a cigarette.*]

KILROY: No thanks.

GYPSY: Come on, indulge yourself. You got nothing to lose that won't be lost.

KILROY: If that's a professional opinion, I don't respect it.

GYPSY: Resume your seat and give me your full name.

KILROY: Kilroy.

GYPSY [*writing all this down*]: Date of birth and place of that disaster?

KILROY: Both unknown.

GYPSY: Address?

KILROY: Traveler.

GYPSY: Parents?

KILROY: Anonymous.

GYPSY: Who brought you up?

KILROY: I was brought up and down by an eccentric old aunt in Dallas.

GYPSY: Raise both hands simultaneously and swear that you have not come here for the purpose of committing an unmoral act.

ESMERALDA [*from off stage*]: Hey, Chico!

GYPSY: *QUIET!* Childhood diseases?

KILROY: Whooping cough, measles and mumps.

GYPSY: Likes and dislikes?

KILROY: I like situations I can get out of. I don't like cops and—

GYPSY: Immaterial! Here! Signature on this!

[*She hands him a blank.*]

KILROY: What is it?

GYPSY: You always sign something, don't you?

KILROY: Not till I know what it is.

GYPSY: It's just a little formality to give a tone to the establishment and make an impression on our out-of-town trade. Roll up your sleeve.

KILROY: What for?

GYPSY: A shot of some kind.

KILROY: What kind?

GYPSY: Any kind. Don't they always give you some kind of a shot?

KILROY: "They"?

GYPSY: Brass hats, Americanos!

[*She injects a hypo.*]

KILROY: I am no guinea pig!

GYPSY: Don't kid yourself. We're all of us guinea pigs in the laboratory of God. Humanity is just a work in progress.

KILROY: I don't make it out.

GYPSY: Who does? The Camino Real is a funny paper read backward!

[*There is weird piping outside. Kilroy shifts on his seat. The Gypsy grins.*]

Tired? The altitude makes you sleepy?

KILROY: It makes me nervous.

GYPSY: I'll show you how to take a slug of tequila! It dilates the capillaries. First you sprinkle salt on the back of your hand. Then lick it off with your tongue. Now then you toss the shot down!

[*She demonstrates.*]

—And then you bite into the lemon. That way it goes down easy, but what a bang! —You're next.

KILROY: No, thanks, I'm on the wagon.

GYPSY: There's an old Chinese proverb that says, "When your goose is cooked you might as well have it cooked with plenty of gravy."

[*She laughs.*]

Get up, baby. Let's have a look at yuh!—You're not a bad-looking boy. Sometimes working for the Yankee dollar isn't a painful profession. Have you ever been attracted by older women?

KILROY: Frankly, no, ma'am.

GYPSY: Well, there's a first time for everything.

KILROY: That is a subject I cannot agree with you on.

GYPSY: You think I'm an old bag?

[*Kilroy laughs awkwardly. The Gypsy slaps his face.*]

Will you take the cards or the crystal?

KILROY: It's immaterial.

GYPSY: All right, we'll begin with the cards.

[*She shuffles and deals.*]

Ask me a question.

KILROY: Has my luck run out?

GYPSY: Baby, your luck ran out the day you were born. Another question.

KILROY: Ought I to leave this town?

GYPSY: It don't look to me like you've got much choice in the matter . . . Take a card.

[*Kilroy takes one.*]

GYPSY: Ace?

KILROY: Yes, ma'am.

GYPSY: What color?

KILROY: Black.

GYPSY: Oh, oh—That does it. How big is your heart?

KILROY: As big as the head of a baby.

GYPSY: It's going to break.

KILROY: That's what I was afraid of.

GYPSY: The Streetcleaners are waiting for you outside the door.

KILROY: Which door, the front one? I'll slip out the back!

GYPSY: Leave us face it frankly, your number is up! You must've known a long time that the name of Kilroy was on the Streetcleaners' list.

KILROY: Sure. But not on top of it!

GYPSY: It's always a bit of a shock. Wait a minute! Here's good news. The Queen of Hearts has turned up in proper position.

KILROY: What's that mean?

GYPSY: Love, baby!

KILROY: Love?

GYPSY: The Booby Prize! —Esmeralda!

[*She rises and hits a gong. A divan is carried out. The Gypsy's Daughter is seated in a reclining position, like an odalisque, on this low divan. A spangled veil covers her face. From this veil to the girdle below her navel, that supports her diaphanous bifurcated skirt, she is nude except for a pair of glittering emerald snakes coiled over her breasts. Kilroy's head moves in a dizzy circle and a canary warbles inside it.*]

KILROY: WHAT'S—WHAT'S *HER* SPECIALTY?—Tea leaves?

[*The Gypsy wags a finger.*]

GYPSY: You know what curiosity did to the tomcat!—Nursie, give me my glamor wig and my forty-five. I'm hitting the street! I gotta go down to Walgreen's for change.

KILROY: What change?

GYPSY: The change from that ten-spot you're about to give me.

NURSIE: Don't argue with her. She has a will of iron.

KILROY: I'm not arguing!

[*He reluctantly produces the money.*]

But let's be *fair* about this! I hocked my golden gloves for this sawbuck!

NURSIE: All of them Yankee bastids want something for nothing!

KILROY: I want a receipt for this bill.

NURSIE: No one is gypped at the Gypsy's!

KILROY: That's wonderful! How do I know it?

GYPSY: It's in the cards, it's in the crystal ball, it's in the tea leaves! Absolutely no one is gypped at the Gypsy's!

[*She snatches the bill. The wind howls.*]

Such changeable weather! I'll slip on my summer furs! Nursie, break out my summer furs!

NURSIE [*leering grotesquely*]: *Mink or sable?*

GYPSY: *Ha ha, that's a doll!* Here! Clock him!

[*Nursie tosses her a greasy blanket, and the Gypsy tosses Nursie an alarm clock. The Gypsy rushes through the beaded string curtains.*]

Adios! Ha ha!!

[*She is hardly offstage when two shots ring out. Kilroy starts.*]

ESMERALDA [*plaintively*]: Mother has such an awful time on the street.

KILROY: You mean that she is insulted on the street?

ESMERALDA: By strangers.

KILROY [*to the audience*]: I shouldn't think acquaintances would do it.

[*She curls up on the low divan. Kilroy licks his lips.*]

—You seem very different from—this afternoon . . .

ESMERALDA: This afternoon?

KILROY: Yes, in the plaza when I was being roughed up by them gorillas and you was being dragged in the house by your Mama!

[*Esmeralda stares at him blandly.*]

You don't remember?

ESMERALDA: I never remember what happened before the moon-rise makes me a virgin.

KILROY: —That—comes as a shock to you, huh?

ESMERALDA: Yes. It comes as a shock.

KILROY [*smiling*]: You have a little temporary amnesia they call it!

ESMERALDA: Yankee . . .

KILROY: Huh?

ESMERALDA: I'm glad I chose you. I'm glad that you were chosen.

[*Her voice trails off.*]

I'm glad. I'm very glad . . .

NURSIE: Doll!

ESMERALDA: —What is it, Nursie?

NURSIE: How are things progressing?

ESMERALDA: Slowly, Nursie—

[*Nursie comes lumbering in.*]

NURSIE: I want some light reading matter.

ESMERALDA: He's sitting on *Screen Secrets.*

KILROY [*jumping up*]: Aw. Here.

[*He hands her the fan magazine. She lumbers back out, coyly.*]

—I—I feel——self-conscious . . .

[*He suddenly jerks out a silver-framed photo.*]

—D'you—like pictures?

ESMERALDA: Moving pictures?

KILROY: No, a—motionless—snapshot!

ESMERALDA: Of you?

KILROY: Of my—real—true woman . . . She was a platinum blonde the same as Jean Harlow. Do you remember Jean Harlow? No, you wouldn't remember Jean Harlow. It shows you are getting old when you remember Jean Harlow.

[*He puts the snapshot away.*]

. . . They say that Jean Harlow's ashes are kept in a little private cathedral in Forest Lawn . . . Wouldn't it be wonderful if you could sprinkle them ashes over the ground like seeds, and out of each one would spring another Jean Harlow? And when spring comes you could just walk out and pick them off the bush! . . . You don't talk much.

ESMERALDA: You want me to *talk*?

KILROY: Well, that's the way we do things in the States. A little vino, some records on the Victrola, some quiet conversation—and then if both parties are in a mood for romance . . . Romance—

ESMERALDA: Music!

[*She rises and pours some wine from a slender crystal decanter as music is heard.*]

They say that the monetary system has got to be stabilized all over the world.

KILROY [*taking the glass*]: Repeat that, please. My radar was not wide open.

ESMERALDA: I said that *they* said that—uh, skip it! But we couldn't care less as long as we keep on getting the Yankee dollar . . . plus federal tax!

KILROY: That's for surely!

ESMERALDA: How do you feel about the class struggle? Do you take sides in that?

KILROY: Not that I—

ESMERALDA: Neither do we because of the dialectics.

KILROY: Who! Which?

ESMERALDA: Languages with accents, I suppose. But Mama don't care as long as they don't bring the Pope over here and put him in the White House.

KILROY: Who would do that?

ESMERALDA: Oh, the Bolsheviskies, those nasty old things with whiskers! *Whiskers scratch!* But little moustaches tickle . . .

[*She giggles.*]

KILROY: I always got a smooth shave . . .

ESMERALDA: And how do you feel about the Mumbo Jumbo? Do you think they've got the Old Man in the bag yet?

KILROY: The Old Man?

ESMERALDA: God. We don't think so. We think there has been so much of the Mumbo Jumbo it's put Him to sleep!

[*Kilroy jumps up impatiently.*]

KILROY: This is not what I mean by a quiet conversation. I mean this is no where! *No where!*

ESMERALDA: What sort of talk do you want?

KILROY: Something more—intimate sort of! You know, like—

ESMERALDA: —Where did you get those eyes?

KILROY: *PERSONAL! Yeah* . . .

ESMERALDA: Well,—where did you get those eyes?

KILROY: Out of a dead codfish!

NURSIE [*shouting offstage*]: DOLL!

[*Kilroy springs up, pounding his left palm with his right fist.*]

ESMERALDA: What?

NURSIE: Fifteen minutes!

KILROY: I'm no hot-rod mechanic. [*To the audience:*] I bet she's out there holding a stop watch to see that I don't overstay my time in this place!

ESMERALDA [*calling through the string curtains*]: *Nursie, go to bed, Nursie!*

KILROY [*in a fierce whisper*]: That's right, go to bed, Nursie!!

[*There is a loud crash offstage.*]

ESMERALDA: —Nursie has gone to bed . . .

[*She drops the string curtains and returns to the alcove.*]

KILROY [*with vast relief*]: —Ahhhhhhhhhh . . .

ESMERALDA: What've you got your eyes on?

KILROY: Those green snakes on you—what do you wear them for?

ESMERALDA: Supposedly for protection, but really for fun.

[*He crosses to the divan.*]

What are you going to do?

KILROY: I'm about to establish a beachhead on that sofa.

[*He sits down.*]

How about—lifting your veil?

ESMERALDA: I can't lift it.

KILROY: Why not?

ESMERALDA: I promised Mother I wouldn't.

KILROY: I thought your mother was the broad-minded type.

ESMERALDA: Oh, she is, but you know how mothers are. You can lift it for me, if you say pretty please.

KILROY: Aww——

ESMERALDA: Go on, say it! Say pretty please!

KILROY: No!!

ESMERALDA: Why not?

KILROY: It's silly.

ESMERALDA: Then you can't lift my veil!

KILROY: Oh, all right. Pretty please.

ESMERALDA: Say it again!

KILROY: Pretty please.

ESMERALDA: Now say it once more like you meant it.

[*He jumps up. She grabs his hand.*]

Don't go away.

KILROY: You're making a fool out of me.

ESMERALDA: I was just teasing a little. Because you're so cute. Sit down again, please—*pretty* please!

[*He falls on the couch.*]

KILROY: What is that wonderful perfume you've got on?

ESMERALDA: Guess!

KILROY: Chanel Number Five?

ESMERALDA: No.

KILROY: Tabu?

ESMERALDA: No.

KILROY: I give up.

ESMERALDA: It's *Noche en Acapulco*! I'm just dying to go to Acapulco. I wish that you would take me to Acapulco.

[*He sits up.*]

What's the matter?

KILROY: You Gypsies' daughters are invariably reminded of something without which you cannot do—just when it looks like everything has been fixed.

ESMERALDA: That isn't nice at all. I'm not the gold-digger type. Some girls see themselves in silver foxes. I only see myself in Acapulco!

KILROY: At Todd's Place?

ESMERALDA: Oh, no, at the Mirador! Watching those pretty boys dive off the Quebrada!

KILROY Look again, baby. Maybe you'll see yourself in Paramount Pictures or having a Singapore Sling at a Statler bar!

ESMERALDA: You're being sarcastic?

KILROY: Nope. Just realistic. All of you Gypsies' daughters have hearts of stone, and I'm not whistling "Dixie"! But just the same, the night before a man dies, he says, "Pretty please—will you let me lift your veil?"—while the Streetcleaners wait for him right outside the door!—because to be warm for a little longer is life. And love?—that's a four-letter word which is sometimes no better than one you see printed on fences by kids playing hooky from school!—Oh, well— what's the use of complaining? You Gypsies' daughters have ears that only catch sounds like the snap of a gold cigarette case! Or, pretty please, baby,—we're going to Acapulco!

ESMERALDA: *Are* we?

KILROY: See what I mean? [*To the audience:*] Didn't I tell you?! [*To Esmeralda:*] Yes! In the morning!

ESMERALDA: Ohhhh! I'm dizzy with joy! My little heart is going pitty-pat!

KILROY: My big heart is going boom-boom! Can I lift your veil now?

ESMERALDA: If you will be gentle.

KILROY: I would not hurt a fly unless it had on leather mittens.

[*He touches a corner of her spangled veil.*]

ESMERALDA: Ohhh . . .

KILROY: What?

ESMERALDA: Ohhhhhh!!

KILROY: Why! What's the matter?

ESMERALDA: You are not being gentle!

KILROY: I *am* being gentle.

ESMERALDA: You are *not* being gentle.

KILROY: What was I being, then?

ESMERALDA: Rough!

KILROY: I am *not* being rough.

ESMERALDA: Yes, you *are* being rough. You have to be gentle with me because you're the first.

KILROY: Are you kidding?

ESMERALDA: No.

KILROY: How about all of those other fiestas you've been to?

ESMERALDA: Each one's the first one. That is the wonderful thing about Gypsies' daughters!

KILROY: You can say that again!

ESMERALDA: I don't like you when you're like that.

KILROY: Like what?

ESMERALDA: Cynical and sarcastic.

KILROY: I am sincere.

ESMERALDA: Lots of boys aren't sincere.

KILROY: Maybe they aren't but I am.

ESMERALDA: Everyone says he's sincere, but everyone isn't sincere. If everyone was sincere who says he's sincere there wouldn't be half so many insincere ones in the world and there would be lots, lots, lots more really sincere ones!

KILROY: I think you have got something there. But how about Gypsies' daughters?

ESMERALDA: Huh?

KILROY: Are they one hundred per cent in the really sincere category?

ESMERALDA: Well, yes, and no, mostly no! But some of them are for a while if their sweethearts are gentle.

KILROY: Would you believe I am sincere and gentle?

ESMERALDA: I would believe that you believe that you are . . . For a while . . .

KILROY: Everything's for a while. For a while is the stuff that dreams are made of, Baby! Now?—Now?

ESMERALDA: Yes, now, but be gentle!—*gentle . . .*

[*He delicately lifts a corner of her veil. She utters a soft cry. He lifts it further. She cries out again. A bit further . . . He turns the spangled veil all the way up from her face.*]

KILROY: I am sincere.

ESMERALDA: I am sincere.

KILROY: I am sincere.

ESMERALDA: I am sincere.

KILROY: I am sincere.

ESMERALDA: I am sincere.

KILROY: I am sincere.

ESMERALDA: I am sincere.

[*Kilroy leans back, removing his hand from her veil. She opens her eyes.*]

Is that all?

KILROY: I am tired.

ESMERALDA: —Already?

[*He rises and goes down the steps from the alcove.*]

KILROY: I am tired, and full of regret . . .

ESMERALDA: Oh!

KILROY: It wasn't much to give my golden gloves for.

ESMERALDA: You pity yourself?

KILROY: That's right, I pity myself and everybody that goes to the Gypsy's daughter. I pity the world and I pity the God who made it.

[*He sits down.*]

ESMERALDA: It's always like that as soon as the veil is lifted. They're all so ashamed of having degraded themselves, and their hearts have more regret than a heart can hold!

KILROY: Even a heart that's as big as the head of a baby!

ESMERALDA: You don't even notice how pretty my face is, do you?

KILROY: You look like all Gypsies' daughters, no better, no worse. But as long as you get to go to Acapulco, your cup runneth over with ordinary contentment.

ESMERALDA: —I've never been so insulted in all my life!

KILROY: Oh, yes, you have, baby. And you'll be insulted worse if you stay in this racket. You'll be insulted so much that it will get to be like water off *a duck's back!*

[*The door slams. Curtains are drawn apart on the Gypsy. Esmeralda lowers her veil hastily. Kilroy pretends not to notice the Gypsy's entrance. She picks up a little bell and rings it over his head.*]

Okay, Mamacita! I am aware of your presence!

GYPSY: Ha-ha! I was followed three blocks by some awful man!

KILROY: Then you caught him.

GYPSY: Naw, he ducked into a subway! I waited fifteen minutes outside the men's room and he never came out!

KILROY: Then you went in?

GYPSY: No! I got myself a sailor!—The streets are brilliant! . . . Have you all been good children?

[*Esmeralda makes a whimpering sound.*]

The pussy will play while the old mother cat is away?

KILROY: Your sense of humor is wonderful, but how about my change, Mamacita?

GYPSY: What change are you talking about?

KILROY: Are you boxed out of your mind? The change from that ten-spot you trotted over to Walgreen's?

GYPSY: Ohhhhh—

KILROY: *Oh, what?*

GYPSY [*counting on her fingers*]: Five for the works, one dollar luxury tax, two for the house percentage and two more pour la service!—makes ten! Didn't I tell you?

KILROY: —What kind of a deal is this?

GYPSY [*whipping out a revolver*]: A rugged one, Baby!

ESMERALDA: Mama, don't be unkind!

GYPSY: Honey, the gentleman's friends are waiting outside the door and it wouldn't be nice to detain him! Come on—Get going—Vamoose!

KILROY: Okay, Mamacita! Me voy!

[*He crosses to the beaded string curtains, turns to look at the Gypsy and her daughter. The piping of the Streetcleaners is heard outside.*]

Sincere?—Sure! That's the wonderful thing about Gypsies' daughters!

[*He goes out. Esmeralda raises a wondering fingertip to one eye. Then she cries out:*]

ESMERALDA: Look, Mama! Look, Mama! A tear!

GYPSY: You have been watching television too much . . .

[*She gathers the cards and turns off the crystal ball as—Light fades out on the phony paradise of the Gypsy's.*]

GUTMAN: Block Thirteen on the Camino Real.

[*He exits.*]

In the blackout the Streetcleaners place a barrel in the center and then hide in the Pit.

Kilroy, who enters from the right, is followed by a spotlight. He sees the barrel and the menacing Streetcleaners and then runs to the closed door of the Siete Mares and rings the bell. No one answers. He backs up so he can see the balcony and calls:

KILROY: Mr. Gutman! Just gimme a cot in the lobby. I'll do odd jobs in the morning. I'll be the Patsy again. I'll light my nose sixty times a minute. I'll take pratfalls and assume the position for anybody that drops a dime on the street . . . Have a heart! Have just a LITTLE heart. Please!

[*There is no response from Gutman's balcony. Jacques enters. He pounds his cane once on the pavement.*]

JACQUES: Gutman! Open the door!—*GUTMAN! GUTMAN!*

[*Eva, a beautiful woman, apparently nude, appears on the balcony.*]

GUTMAN [*from inside*]: Eva darling, you're exposing yourself!

[*He appears on the balcony with a portmanteau.*]

JACQUES: What are you doing with my portmanteau?

GUTMAN: Haven't you come for your luggage?

JACQUES: Certainly not! I haven't checked out of here!

GUTMAN: Very few do . . . but residences are frequently terminated.

JACQUES: Open the door!

GUTMAN: Open the letter with the remittance check in it!

JACQUES: In the morning!

GUTMAN: Tonight!

JACQUES: Upstairs in my room!

GUTMAN: Downstairs at the entrance!

JACQUES: I won't be intimidated!

GUTMAN [*raising the portmanteau over his head*]: What?!

JACQUES: Wait!—

[*He takes the letter out of his pocket.*]

Give me some light.

[*Kilroy strikes a match and holds it over Jacques' shoulder.*]

Thank you. What does it say?

GUTMAN: —Remittances?

KILROY [*reading the letter over Jacques' shoulder*]: —discontinued . . .

[*Gutman raises the portmanteau again.*]

JACQUES: Careful, I have—

[*The portmanteau lands with a crash. The Bum comes to the window at the crash. A. Ratt comes out to his doorway at the same time.*]

—fragile—mementos . . .

[*He crosses slowly down to the portmanteau and kneels as . . . Gutman laughs and slams the balcony door. Jacques turns to Kilroy. He smiles at the young adventurer.*]

—"And so at last it has come, the distinguished thing!"

[*A. Ratt speaks as Jacques touches the portmanteau.*]

A. RATT: Hey, Dad—Vacancy here! A bed at the "Ritz Men Only." A little white ship to sail the dangerous night in.

JACQUES: Single or double?

A. RATT: There's only singles in this pad.

JACQUES [*to Kilroy*]: Match you for it.

KILROY: What the hell, we're buddies, we can sleep spoons! If we can't sleep, we'll push the washstand against the door and sing old popular songs till the crack of dawn! . . . "Heart of my heart, I love that melody!" . . . You bet your life I do.

[*Jacques takes out a pocket handkerchief and starts to grasp the portmanteau handle.*]

—It looks to me like you could use a redcap and my rates are nonunion!

[*He picks up the portmanteau and starts to cross toward the "Ritz Men Only." He stops at right center.*]

Sorry, buddy. Can't make it! The altitude on this block has affected my ticker! And in the distance which is nearer than further, I hear— the Streetcleaners'—piping!

[*Piping is heard.*]

JACQUES: COME ALONG!

[*He lifts the portmanteau and starts on.*]

KILROY: NO. Tonight! I prefer! To sleep! Out! Under! The stars!

JACQUES [*gently*]: I understand, Brother!

KILROY [*to Jacques as he continues toward the "Ritz Men Only"*]: Bon Voyage! I hope that you sail the dangerous night to the sweet golden port of morning!

JACQUES [*exiting*]: Thanks, Brother!

KILROY: Excuse the *corn!* I'm sincere!

BUM: Show me the way to go home! . . .

GUTMAN [*appearing on the balcony with white parakeet*]: Block Fourteen on the Camino Real.

At opening, the Bum is still at the window.

The Streetcleaners' piping continues a little louder. Kilroy climbs, breathing heavily, to the top of the stairs and stands looking out at Terra Incognita as . . .

Marguerite enters the plaza through alleyway at right. She is accompanied by a silent Young Man who wears a domino.

MARGUERITE: Don't come any further with me. I'll have to wake the night porter. Thank you for giving me safe conduct through the Medina.

[*She has offered her hand. He grips it with a tightness that makes her wince.*]

Ohhhh . . . I'm not sure which is more provocative in you, your ominous silence or your glittering smile or—

[*He's looking at her purse.*]

What do you want? . . . Oh!

[*She starts to open the purse. He snatches it. She gasps as he suddenly strips her cloak off her. Then he snatches off her pearl necklace. With each successive despoilment, she gasps and retreats but makes no resistance. Her eyes are closed. He continues to smile. Finally, he rips her dress and runs his hands over her body as if to see if she had anything else of value concealed on her.*]

—What else do I have that you want?

THE YOUNG MAN [*contemptuously*]: Nothing.

[*The Young Man exits through the cantina, examining his loot. The Bum leans out his window, draws a deep breath and says:*]

BUM: Lonely.

MARGUERITE [*to herself*]: Lonely . . .

KILROY [*on the steps*]: Lonely . . .

[*The Streetcleaners' piping is heard. Marguerite runs to the Siete Mares and rings the bell. Nobody answers. She crosses to the terrace. Kilroy, meanwhile, has descended the stairs.*]

MARGUERITE: Jacques!

[*Piping is heard.*]

KILROY: Lady?

MARGUERITE: What?

KILROY: —*I'm—safe* . . .

MARGUERITE: I wasn't expecting that music tonight, were you?

[*Piping.*]

KILROY: It's them Streetcleaners.

MARGUERITE: I know.

[*Piping.*]

KILROY: You better go on in, lady.

MARGUERITE: No.

KILROY: GO ON IN!

MARGUERITE: NO! I want to stay out here and I do what I want to do!

[*Kilroy looks at her for the first time.*]

Sit down with me please.

KILROY: They're coming for me. The Gypsy told me I'm on top of their list. Thanks for. Taking my. Hand.

[*Piping is heard.*]

MARGUERITE: Thanks for taking mine.

[*Piping.*]

KILROY: Do me one more favor. Take out of my pocket a picture. My fingers are. Stiff.

MARGUERITE: This one?

KILROY: My one. True. Woman.

MARGUERITE: A silver-framed photo! Was she really so fair?

KILROY: She was so fair and much fairer than they could tint that picture!

MARGUERITE: Then you have been on the street when the street was royal.

KILROY: Yeah . . . when the street was royal!

[*Piping is heard. Kilroy rises.*]

MARGUERITE: Don't get up, don't leave me!

KILROY: I want to be on my feet when the Streetcleaners come for me!

MARGUERITE: Sit back down again and tell me about your girl.

[*He sits.*]

KILROY: Y'know what it is you miss most? When you're separated. From someone. You lived. With. And loved? It's waking up in the night! With that—warmness beside you!

MARGUERITE: Yes, that *warmness* beside you!

KILROY: Once you get used to that. *Warmness!* It's a hell of a lonely feeling to wake up without it! Specially in some dollar-a-night hotel room on Skid! A hot-water bottle won't do. And a stranger. Won't do. It has to be some one you're used to. And that you. *KNOW LOVES* you!

[*Piping is heard.*]

Can you see them?

MARGUERITE: I see no one but you.

KILROY: I looked at my wife one night when she was sleeping and that was the night that the medics wouldn't okay me for no more fights . . . Well . . . My wife was sleeping with a smile like a child's. I kissed her. She didn't wake up. I took a pencil and paper. I wrote her. Good-bye!

MARGUERITE: That was the night she would have loved you the most!

KILROY: Yeah, *that* night, but what about *after* that night? Oh, lady . . . Why should a beautiful girl tie up with a broken-down champ?—The earth still turning and her obliged to turn with it, not out—of dark into light but out of light into dark? Naw, naw, naw, naw!—Washed up!—Finished!

[*Piping.*]

. . . that ain't a word that a man can't look at . . . There ain't no words in the language a man can't look at . . . and know just what they mean. And be. And act. And *go!*

[*He turns to the waiting Streetcleaners.*]

Come on! . . . Come on! . . . COME ON, YOU SONS OF BITCHES! KILROY IS HERE! HE'S READY!

[*A gong sounds. Kilroy swings at the Streetcleaners. They circle about him out of reach, turning him by each of their movements. The swings grow wilder like a boxer. He falls to his knees still swinging and finally collapses flat on his face. The Streetcleaners pounce but La Madrecita throws herself protectingly over the body and covers it with her shawl. Blackout.*]

MARGUERITE: Jacques!

GUTMAN [*on balcony*]: Block Fifteen on the Camino Real.

BLOCK FIFTEEN

La Madrecita is seated; across her knees is the body of Kilroy. Up center, a low table on wheels bears a sheeted figure. Beside the table stands a Medical Instructor addressing Students and Nurses, all in white surgical outfits.

INSTRUCTOR: This is the body of an unidentified vagrant.

LA MADRECITA: This was thy son, America—and now mine.

INSTRUCTOR: He was found in an alley along the Camino Real.

LA MADRECITA: Think of him, now, as he was before his luck failed him. Remember his time of greatness, when he was not faded, not frightened.

INSTRUCTOR: More light, please!

LA MADRECITA: More light!

INSTRUCTOR: Can everyone see clearly!

LA MADRECITA: Everyone must see clearly!

INSTRUCTOR: There is no external evidence of disease.

LA MADRECITA: He had clear eyes and the body of a champion boxer.

INSTRUCTOR: There are no marks of violence on the body.

LA MADRECITA: He had the soft voice of the South and a pair of golden gloves.

INSTRUCTOR: His death was apparently due to natural causes.

[The Students make notes. There are keening voices.]

LA MADRECITA: Yes, blow wind where night thins! He had many admirers!

INSTRUCTOR: There are no legal claimants.

LA MADRECITA: He stood as a planet among the moons of their longing, haughty with youth, a champion of the prize-ring!

INSTRUCTOR: No friends or relatives having identified him—

LA MADRECITA: You should have seen the lovely monogrammed robe in which he strode the aisles of the colosseums!

INSTRUCTOR: After the elapse of a certain number of days, his body becomes the property of the State—

LA MADRECITA: Yes, blow wind where night thins—for laurel is not everlasting . . .

INSTRUCTOR: And now is transferred to our hands for the nominal sum of five dollars.

LA MADRECITA: This was thy son,—and now mine . . .

INSTRUCTOR: We will now proceed with the dissection. Knife, please!

LA MADRECITA: Blow wind!

[*Keening is heard offstage.*]

Yes, blow wind where night thins! You are his passing bell and his lamentation.

[*More keening is heard.*]

Keen for him, all maimed creatures, deformed and mutilated—his homeless ghost is your own!

INSTRUCTOR: First we will open up the chest cavity and examine the heart for evidence of coronary occlusion.

LA MADRECITA: His heart was pure gold and as big as the head of a baby.

INSTRUCTOR: We will make an incision along the vertical line.

LA MADRECITA: Rise, ghost! Go! Go bird! "Humankind cannot bear very much reality."

[*At the touch of her flowers, Kilroy stirs and pushes himself up slowly from her lap. On his feet again, he rubs his eyes and looks around him.*]

VOICES [*crying offstage*]: Olé! Olé! Olé!

KILROY Hey! Hey, somebody! Where am I?

[*He notices the dissection room and approaches.*]

INSTRUCTOR [*removing a glittering sphere from a dummy corpse*]: Look at this heart. It's as big as the head of a baby.

KILROY: My heart!

INSTRUCTOR: Wash it off so we can look for the pathological lesions.

KILROY: Yes, siree, that's my heart!

GUTMAN: Block Sixteen!

[*Kilroy pauses just outside the dissection area as a Student takes the heart and dips it into a basin on the stand beside the table. The Student suddenly cries out and holds aloft a glittering gold sphere.*]

INSTRUCTOR: Look! This heart's solid gold!

BLOCK SIXTEEN

KILROY [*rushing forward*]: That's mine, you bastards!

[*He snatches the golden sphere from the Medical Instructor. The autopsy proceeds as if nothing had happened as the spot of light on the table fades out, but for Kilroy a ghostly chase commences, a dreamlike re-enactment of the chase that occurred at the end of Block Six. Gutman shouts from his balcony:*]

GUTMAN: Stop, thief, stop, corpse! That gold heart is the property of the State! Catch him, catch the golden-heart robber!

[*Kilroy dashes offstage into an aisle of the theatre. There is the wail of a siren: the air is filled with calls and whistles, roar of motors, screeching brakes, pistol-shots, thundering footsteps. The dimness of the auditorium is transected by searching rays of light—but there are no visible pursuers.*]

KILROY [*as he runs panting up the aisle*]: This is my heart! It don't belong to no State, not even the U.S.A. Which way is out? Where's the Greyhound depot? Nobody's going to put my heart in a bottle in a museum and charge admission to support the rotten police! Where are they? Which way are they going? Or coming? Hey, somebody, help me get out of here! Which way do I—which way—which way do I—go! go! go! go! go!

[*He has now arrived in the balcony.*]

Gee, I'm lost! I don't know where I am! I'm all turned around, I'm confused, I don't understand—what's—happened, it's like a—*dream,* it's—just like a—dream . . . *Mary! Oh, Mary! Mary!*

[*He has entered the box from which he leapt in Block Two. A clear shaft of light falls on him. He looks up into it, crying:*]

Mary, help a Christian!! Help a Christian, Mary!—It's like a dream . . .

[*Esmeralda appears in a childish nightgown beside her gauze-tented bed on the Gypsy's roof. Her Mother appears with a cup of some sedative drink, cooing . . .*]

108

GYPSY: Beddy-bye, beddy-bye, darling. It's sleepy-time down South and up North, too, and also East and West!

KILROY [*softly*]: Yes, it's—like *a—dream* . . .

[*He leans panting over the ledge of the box, holding his heart like a football, watching Esmeralda.*]

GYPSY: Drink your Ovaltine, Ducks, and the sandman will come on tiptoe with a bag full of dreams . . .

ESMERALDA: I want to dream of the Chosen Hero, Mummy.

GYPSY: Which one, the one that's coming or the one that is gone?

ESMERALDA: The *only* one, *Kilroy!* He was *sincere!*

KILROY: That's *right! I was,* for a while!

GYPSY: How do you know that Kilroy was sincere?

ESMERALDA: He said so.

KILROY: That's the truth, I *was!*

GYPSY: When did he say that?

ESMERALDA: When he lifted my veil.

GYPSY: Baby, they're always sincere when they lift your veil; it's one of those natural reflexes that don't mean a thing.

KILROY [*aside*]: What a cynical old bitch that Gypsy mama is!

GYPSY: And there's going to be lots of other fiestas for you, baby doll, and lots of other chosen heroes to lift your little veil when Mamacita and Nursie are out of the room.

ESMERALDA: No, Mummy, never, I mean it!

KILROY: I *believe* she means it!

GYPSY: Finish your Ovaltine and say your Now-I-Lay-Me.

[*Esmeralda sips the drink and hands her the cup.*]

KILROY [*with a catch in his voice*]: I had one true woman, which I can't go back to, but now I've found another.

[He leaps onto the stage from the box.]

ESMERALDA [*dropping to her knees*]: Now I lay me down to sleep, I pray the Lord my soul to keep. If I should die before I wake, I pray the Lord my soul to take.

GYPSY: God bless Mummy!

ESMERALDA: And the crystal ball and the tea leaves.

KILROY: *Pssst!*

ESMERALDA: What's that?

GYPSY: A tomcat in the plaza.

ESMERALDA: God bless all cats without pads in the plaza tonight.

KILROY: Amen!

[He falls to his knees in the empty plaza.]

ESMERALDA: God bless all con men and hustlers and pitch-men who hawk their hearts on the street, all two-time losers who're likely to lose once more, the courtesan who made the mistake of love, the greatest of lovers crowned with the longest horns, the poet who wandered far from his heart's green country and possibly will and possibly won't be able to find his way back, look down with a smile tonight on the last cavaliers, the ones with the rusty armor and soiled white plumes, and visit with understanding and something that's almost tender those fading legends that come and go in this plaza like songs not clearly remembered, oh, sometime and somewhere, let there be something to mean the word *honor* again!

QUIXOTE [*hoarsely and loudly, stirring slightly among his verminous rags*]: Amen!

KILROY: Amen . . .

GYPSY [*disturbed*]: —That will do, now.

ESMERALDA: *And, oh, God, let me dream tonight of the Chosen Hero!*

GYPSY: Now, sleep. Fly away on the magic carpet of dreams!

[*Esmeralda crawls into the gauze-tented cot. The Gypsy descends from the roof.*]

KILROY: Esmeralda My little Gypsy sweetheart!

ESMERALDA [*sleepily*]: Go away, cat.

[*The light behind the gauze is gradually dimming.*]

KILROY: This is no cat. This is the chosen hero of the big fiesta, Kilroy, the champion of the golden gloves with his gold heart cut from his chest and in his hands to give you!

ESMERALDA: Go away. Let me dream of the Chosen Hero.

KILROY: What a hassle! Mistook for a cat! What can I do to convince this doll I'm real?

[*Three brass balls wink brilliantly.*]

—Another transaction seems to be indicated!

[*He rushes to the Loan Shark's. The entrance immediately lights up.*]

My heart is gold! What will you give me for it?

[*Jewels, furs, sequined gowns, etc., are tossed to his feet. He throws his heart like a basketball to the Loan Shark, snatches up the loot and rushes back to the Gypsy's.*]

Doll! Behold this loot! I gave my golden heart for it!

ESMERALDA: Go away, cat . . .

[*She falls asleep. Kilroy bangs his forehead with his fist, then rushes to the Gypsy's door, pounds it with both fists. The door is thrown open and the sordid contents of a large jar are thrown at him. He falls back gasping, spluttering, retching. He retreats and finally assumes an exaggerated attitude of despair.*]

KILROY: Had for a button! Stewed, screwed and tattooed on the Camino Real! Baptized, finally, with the contents of a slop-jar!—Did anybody say the deal was rugged?!

[*Quixote stirs against the wall of Skid Row. He hawks and spits and staggers to his feet.*]

GUTMAN: Why, the old knight's awake, his dream is over!

QUIXOTE [to Kilroy]: Hello! Is that a fountain?

KILROY: —Yeah, but—

QUIXOTE: I've got a mouthful of old chicken feathers . . .

[He approaches the fountain. It begins to flow. Kilroy falls back in amazement as the Old Knight rinses his mouth and drinks and removes his jacket to bathe, handing the tattered garment to Kilroy.]

QUIXOTE [as he bathes]: Qué pasa, mi amigo?

KILROY: The deal is rugged. D'you know what I mean?

QUIXOTE: Who knows better than I what a rugged deal is!

[He produces a toothbrush and brushes his teeth.]

—Will you take some advice?

KILROY: Brother, at this point on the Camino I will take anything which is offered!

QUIXOTE: Don't Pity! Your! Self!

[He takes out a pocket mirror and grooms his beard and moustache.]

The wounds of the vanity, the many offenses our egos have to endure, being housed in bodies that age and hearts that grow tired, are better accepted with a tolerant smile—like this!—You see?

[He cracks his face in two with an enormous grin.]

GUTMAN: Follow-spot on the face of the ancient knight!

QUIXOTE: Otherwise what you become is a bag full of curdled cream—leche mala, we call it!—attractive to nobody, least of all to yourself!

[He passes the comb and pocket mirror to Kilroy.]

Have you got any plans?

KILROY [a bit uncertainly, wistfully]: Well, I was thinking of—going on from—here!

QUIXOTE: Good! Come with me.

KILROY [*to the audience*]: Crazy old bastard. [*Then to the Knight:*] Donde?

QUIXOTE [*starting for the stairs*]: Quien sabe!

[*The fountain is now flowing loudly and sweetly. The Street People are moving toward it with murmurs of wonder. Marguerite comes out upon the terrace.*]

KILROY: Hey, there's—!

QUIXOTE: Shhh! Listen!

[*They pause on the stairs.*]

MARGUERITE: Abdullah!

[*Gutman has descended to the terrace.*]

GUTMAN: Mademoiselle, allow me to deliver the message for you. It would be in bad form if I didn't take some final part in the pageant.

[*He crosses the plaza to the opposite façade and shouts "Casanova!" under the window of the "Ritz Men Only." Meanwhile Kilroy scratches out the verb "is" and prints the correction "was" in the inscription on the ancient wall.*]

Casanova! Great lover and King of Cuckolds on the Camino Real! The last of your ladies has guaranteed your tabs and is expecting you for breakfast on the terrace!

[*Casanova looks first out of the practical window of the flophouse, then emerges from its scabrous doorway, haggard, unshaven, crumpled in dress but bearing himself as erectly as ever. He blinks and glares fiercely into the brilliant morning light. Marguerite cannot return his look, she averts her face with a look for which anguish would not be too strong a term, but at the same time she extends a pleading hand toward him. After some hesitation, he begins to move toward her, striking the pavement in measured cadence with his cane, glancing once, as he crosses, out at the audience with a wry smile that makes admissions that would be embarrassing to a vainer man than Casanova now is. When he reaches Marguerite*] *she gropes for his hand, seizes it with a low cry and presses it spasmodically to her lips while he draws her into his arms and looks above her sobbing, dyed-golden head with the serene, clouded gaze of someone mortally ill as the mercy of a narcotic laps over his pain. Quixote raises his lance in a formal gesture and cries out hoarsely, powerfully from the stairs:*]

QUIXOTE: *The violets in the mountains have broken the rocks!*

[*Quixote goes through the arch with Kilroy.*]

GUTMAN [*to the audience*]: The Curtain Line has been spoken! [*To the wings:*] Bring it down!

[*He bows with a fat man's grace as—*]

THE CURTAIN FALLS.

TEN BLOCKS ON THE CAMINO REAL*

A FANTASY

*Use Anglicized pronunciation: ca'-mino re'-al. (TW)

CHARACTERS

KILROY   25, a vagrant, former boxer
MARGUERITE GAUTIER
JACQUES CASANOVA
BARON DE CHARLUS
MR. GUTMAN   Proprietor of the Siete Mares
THE GYPSY
HER DAUGHTER, ESMERALDA
DON QUIXOTE
SANCHO PANZA
LA MADRECITA DE LAS SOLEDADAS Flower vendor
AN OFFICER
A PEASANT
A SINGER
A GUITAR PLAYER
A CHORUS OF ABOUT TEN DANCERS
TWO STREET-CLEANERS

The Place is ostensibly a small tropical port of the Americas.
   The audience faces a little plaza. It should have grace and mystery and sadness: that peculiar dreamlike feeling that emanates from such squares in Mexico and from the popular songs of that country. In full light it suggests a drawing in pastels, with the chalky white of adobe walls and the delicate tints of rain-washed and sun-bleached posters. The plaza is contained by three street-façades and in its center is a shallow dried-up fountain. Along the back of plaza, parallel to the proscenium, is El Camino Real *designated by a street-sign. On this is the central playing area, The Gypsy's Establishment, the facing wall of which is a transparency that is lifted for an interior scene. On this transparency painted, a sign:* HOY! NOCHE DE FIESTA! THE MOON WILL RESTORE THE VIRGINITY OF MY DAUGHTER!! *(this being in Spanish). The entrance to the establishment is on the narrow cobbled alley that issues upstage from the (stage) left side of the plaza. This alley is steep as a flight of stairs (such alleys are common in mountain villages of Mexico) and it climbs to a crumbling yellow arch level with the roof of the Gypsy's. Perched on the arch is a carrion bird; beyond it, and over the roofs of the village, is a vista of country like a landscape on the moon which extends to a range of blue and white mountains. The alley has a sign that says:* THIS WAY OUT.
   On the right is the Siete Mares *hotel façade and portico and the entrance to its cantina. This façade is designed for first class tourist-trade. The walls are turquoise and decorated with devices of the sea, such as star-fish and conch-shells and leaping dolphins. Before the hotel is a small round table and two chairs, both of graceful white iron-work. On the opposite side of the plaza is the door and window of a pawn-shop, frankly called* THE LOAN SHARK. *Over it three yellow balls.*
   As the curtain rises there are stationary figures about the plaza. These figures will be variously used as vendors, dancers and chorus of the "Laboratory" scene. A group of ten dancers would suffice for all chorus uses. They are crouching, leaning and lying about the plaza in their dust-colored rags. They have a look of immense torpor as if they were stunned or drugged by the great ball of fire that rolls gradually over the nameless town and country. One of the street-figures is distinct from the others. She is an ancient woman who wears a snow-

white rebozo and who is vending those glittering and gaudy flowers made of tin that are used at peasant funerals in the Latin Americas. Her voice is softer and more musical than the others, and her face remains hidden by the blanket until the "Laboratory" scene when she becomes La Madrecita de las Soledadas. Seated by fountain or base of alley.

Also distinct from the others is a guitar player whose instrument is blue: he is dressed as a Mexican street-musician, though he may wear a domino to indicate he is somewhat outside the play, being a sort of master of ceremonies. The guitar and singing may be used at more points than are indicated in the script: the same is true of dancing; though it should not impede a lively progress of scenes. Lightness and quickness should be the keynote of the production: that is, in physical movement, except where otherwise indicated.

Only the guitar player stands erect as the curtain rises. He strikes a sombre chord.

BLOCK I

At this signal a cry is heard. A figure in rags, skin blackened by the sun, tumbles crazily through the arch and down the steep alley to the fountain. There he throws himself on his stomach and thrusts both hands into the dried basin. He staggers to his feet and gives a despairing cry.

FIGURE: *La fuente esta seca!* [*Castanets click mysteriously among the muffled figures. Music comes from the entrance of the cantina. The thirst-crazed peasant turns that way.*]

THE GUITAR PLAYER [*as if speaking for him*]: The fountain is dry. But there is wine in the cantina of the Siete Mares. The cellars of the hotel are stocked with wine. [*The peasant stumbles toward the hotel. The proprietor steps out, a lordly fat man in a white linen suit, smoking a cigar and fanning himself with a palm leaf fan. As the peasant advances he blows a whistle. A man in military dress steps out of cantina.*]

OFFICER: Go back! [*The man stumbles forward. The officer fires at him. He lowers his hands to his stomach, turns slowly about and staggers to the fountain where he falls in a motionless heap. The pro-prietor and the officer return inside. The Plaza is silent and motionless again.*]

BLOCK II

Someone is heard whistling as he approaches. The sound revives the plaza. Vague movements commence among the street figures; they uncover their baskets and arrange their wares, huaraches, sil-ver, peppers, etc. They begin to murmur almost wordlessly among themselves with the weary sound of pigeons. Another moment and the whistler appears. He is a young American wanderer about twenty-five. He wears dungarees and a skivvy shirt, the pants, faded nearly white from long wear and much washing, fit him as closely as the clothes of sculpture. He has a pair of golden boxing gloves slung about his neck, his belt is ruby and emerald-studded. He enters from stage right, along the Camino Real. Stops before the chalked inscription "KILROY IS COMING." Scratches out "COMING" and prints "HERE."

KILROY [*very genially, to all present*]: Haha! [*Then he walks up to the officer in the dull grey uniform, whose hand tightens on the butt of his revolver as Kilroy approaches him.*] Buenos Dias, Senor. [*No response—barely a glance.*] Habla Inglesia?

OFFICER [*spits, then asks slowly*]: What is it you want?

KILROY: Where is Western Union or Wells-Fargo? I got to send a wire to some friends in the States.

OFFICER: No hay Western Union, no hay Wells-Fargo.

KILROY: That is very peculiar. I never struck a town yet that didn't have one or the other. I just got off a boat. Lousiest frigging tub I ever shipped on, one continual hell it was, all the way up from Rio. And me sick, too. I picked up one of those tropical fevers. No sick-bay on that tub, no doctor, no medicine or nothing, not even one quinine pill, and I was burning up with Christ knows how much fever. I couldn't make them understand I was sick. I got a bad heart, too. I had to retire from the prize ring because of my heart. I was the light heavyweight champion of the West Coast, won these gloves!—before my ticker went bad.—Feel my chest! Go on, feel it! [*He seizes the officer's hand and presses it to his chest.*] Feel it. I've got a heart in my chest as big as the head of a baby. Ha-ha! They stood me in front of a screen that makes you transparent and that's what they seen inside me, a heart in my chest as big as the head of a baby! With something like that you don't need the Gypsy to tell you, "Time is short, Baby—get ready to hitch on wings!" Ha-ha! The medics wouldn't okay me for no more fights, and I was advised to give up smoking and liquor and sex. [*Guitar under softly.*] Ha-ha! To give up sex!—I used to believe a man couldn't live without sex—but he *can*—if he *wants* to! My real true woman, my wife, she would of stuck with me, but it was all spoiled with her being scared and me, too, that a real hard kiss would kill me!—So one night while she was sleeping I wrote her good-bye. . . . Y' know what it is you miss most when you've separated from someone you lived with and loved? It's waking up in the night with that warmness beside you. Once you get used to that warmness, it's a hell of a— [*Plaintive music under.*] —lonely feeling to wake up without it, especially in some dollar-a-night hotel room. Ha-ha! A hot water bottle won't do, and a stranger won't do. It has to be someone you're used to and that you know loves you! [*He notices a lack of attention in the officer; grins.*] No comprendo the lingo? [*Music out.*]

OFFICER. What is it you want?

KILROY [*his spirits visibly flagging*]: Excuse my ignorance but what place is this? What is this country and what is the name of this town? [*Music resumes mysterious. Officer stares at him in a slight, contemptuous smile.*] I know it seems funny of me to ask such a question. Loco! But I was so glad to get off that rotten tub I didn't ask nothing of no one except my pay—and I got short-changed on that. I have trouble counting these pesos or Whatzit-you-call-em. [*Jerks out wallet.*] All-a-this-here. In the States that pile of lettuce would make you a plutocrat!—But I bet you this stuff don't add up to fifty dollars American coin. Ha-ha!

OFFICER [*hollowly—mocking*]: Ha-ha.

KILROY [*uneasily*]: Ha-ha!

OFFICER [*making it sound like a death-rattle*]: Ha-ha-ha-ha-ha. [*He turns and starts in the cantina. Kilroy grabs his arm.*]

KILROY: *Hey!*

OFFICER [*rather fiercely*]: What is it you want?

KILROY [*his spirits visibly flagging*]: What is the name of this country and this town? [*Officer thrusts his elbow in Kilroy's stomach and twists his arm loose with Spanish curse. Kicks the swinging doors open and enters cantina.*] Brass hats are the same everywhere. [*Soon as the officer goes the street people come forward and crowd about Kilroy with their wheedling cries. Light music.*]

STREET PEOPLE: Dulces, dulces! Loteria! Loteria! Recuerdos? Recuerdos? Pastele, cafe con leche!

KILROY: No caree, no caree! [*An indescribably frightful old prostitute creeps up to him and grins nightmarishly.*]

PROSTITUTE: Love? Love?

KILROY: *What* did you say?

PROSTITUTE: *Love?*

KILROY: No, thanks, I have ideals!

THE GYPSY'S LOUDSPEAKER: Are you perplexed by something? Are you tired out and confused? Do you have a fever? [*Kilroy looks around for the source of the voice.*] Do you feel yourself to be spiritually unprepared for the age of exploding atoms? Do you distrust the newspapers? Are you suspicious of governments? Have you arrived at a point on the Camino Real where the walls converge not in the distance but right in front of your nose? Does further progress appear impossible to you? Are you afraid of anything at all? Afraid of your heart-beat? Or the eyes of strangers? Afraid of breathing? Afraid of not breathing? Do you wish that things could be straight and simple again as they were in your childhood? Would you like to go back to Kindy Garden! [*The old prostitute has crept up to Kilroy while he listens. She reaches out to him. At the same time a pickpocket lifts his wallet.*]

KILROY [*catching the whore's wrist*]: Keep y'r hands off me, y' dirty ole bag! No caree putas! No loteria, no dulces, nada—so get away! Vamoose! All of you! Quit picking at me! [*Reaches in his pocket and jerks out a handful of small copper and silver coins which he flings disgustedly down the street. The grotesque people scramble after it with their inhuman cries. Kilroy goes on a few steps—then stops short—feeling the back pocket of his dungarees. Then he lets out a startled cry.*] Robbed! By God, I've been robbed! [*The street people scatter to the walls. Turning furiously from one to another.*] Which of you got my wallet? WHICH of you dirty——? Shhhh——Uh! [*They mumble with gestures of incomprehension. He marches back to entrance to hotel.*] Hey! Officer! Oficial!—General! [*The officer finally lounges out of the shadowy hotel entrance and glances at Kilroy with contempt.*] Tienda? One of them's got my wallet! Picked it out of my pocket while that old whore there was groping me! Don't you comprendo?

OFFICER [*slowly*]: Nobody rob you. You don't have no pesos.

KILROY: Huh?

OFFICER: You just dreaming that you have money. You don't ever have money. Nunca! Nada! [*Spits between his teeth.*] Loco . . . [*Officer crosses to fountain. Kilroy stares at him speechlessly for a moment, then bawls out.*]

KILROY: We'll see what the American Embassy says about this! I'll go to the American Consul! I'll have you all—locked up! Jail! Calaboose! The whole—kit and kaboodle of yuh—dirty—ole—tramps—whores! Leeches! Zopilotes! Snakes!

OFFICER [*stopping by the frightful prostitute*]: Pssst! Rosita! [*Jerks his head toward the cantina. She grins horribly and follows him into it. Exhausted by his emotion, Kilroy leans against wall by hotel. Clutches his pounding heart and pulls out a crumpled blue bandanna to swab his forehead and throat.*]

KILROY: Whew! This deal is rugged! Yes, baby—a rugged deal! [*He slowly crosses the Plaza and goes into the entrance beneath the three brass balls, loosening his ruby and emerald studded belt.*]

BLOCK III

There is a fading of light. First dusk falls on the plaza with an effect of coolness. At some distance a woman begins to sing.

WOMAN: "Noche de ronda,
    Que triste pase,
    Que triste cruza—
    Por mi balcon!"

[*The guitar player steps suddenly forward and sweeps his strings.*]

PLAYER: The presence of women has softened the speech of the city! [*From inside the Siete Mares there is a rich peal of male laughter. The proprietor steps out upon the street. He is an august gentleman in a light tropical suit, a black string tie, a pith helmet. His voice and manner are suave and unctuous.*]

PROPRIETOR: Forty pesos a day, American plan. We serve distilled water and have the best wine-cellar in the tropics. We provide for the comfort of our guests, but not their safety. Their jewels and valuables should be deposited with the cashier. Acqui se habla Ingles! Ha-ha-ha! [*He takes out a big gold watch and stares at it fondly. The guitar player strums softly. Proprietor, looking up slowly.*] They are selling the lottery on San Juan de Latrene.

PLAYER: And on the Camino Real.

PROPRIETOR: The girls in the Panama clip-joints are drinking Blue Moons, the gobs and the sea-going bell-hops are getting stewed, screwed and tattooed, and the S. P.'s are busy as cats on a hot tin-roof! Ha ha!—On South Rampart Street and Market Street and Beale Street and Main Street, the nickelodeons and the slot-machines are doing a land-office business. Also the silver screens and the no-cover-charge cantinas, for all work and no play makes Jack a poor jerk who will not get to first base with Jill!

PLAYER: On the Camino Real.

PROPRIETOR: That's right, on the Camino Real! Ha-ha!—You know, to believe in luxury isn't necessarily nor even probably to lack dynamism—

PLAYER: On the Camino Real.

PROPRIETOR: For lots of babies who've never been properly weaned from Hotel Statler room-service, can still make sing or make like magnificent singing—canaries in bed-springs! Ha-ha!

PLAYER: On the Camino Real.

PROPRIETOR: That's right, on the Camino Real!—And in the Loop of Chicago—why, that's the way the crow flies between kids' giggles and light-hearted cohabitation. But, oh, I can tell you!—I have seen them all and known them all and done them all out of their last lucky dollar! Ha-ha!

PLAYER: On the Camino Real.

PROPRIETOR: There's a sort of magnificence in my kind of a robber! I'm a silk-glove artist, and absolutely sincere!

PLAYER: On the Camino Real?

PROPRIETOR: Yes, on the Camino Real! Ha-ha! And my death will be like the fall of a capital city, the sack of Rome or the destruction of Carthage— And, oh, the memories that will go up in smoke! And you mean to tell me that all this flesh will be lost? Ha-ha! It's a joke! I don't for one moment believe you! But still the street-cleaners have given me sidelong glances, which I pretend to ignore.

PLAYER: On the Camino Real.

PROPRIETOR: For I am the owner of the Siete Mares!

PLAYER: On the Camino Real. [*Music changes to lyrical.*]

PROPRIETOR [*with an airy gesture*]: In Yboe City the five-point standards are lit. In Guadalajara the colonnades of the plaza are filled with a murmur of girls vending soft-colored drinks, and girls in the tolerant zones are saying the words that pass for love-poems—

PLAYER: On the Camino Real.

PROPRIETOR [*soberly*]: But there is a moment when we look into ourselves and ask with a wonder which never is lost altogether: Can this be all? Is this it? Is this what the glittering wheels of the heavens turn for? [*Then he leans forward as if conveying a secret.*] Ask the

Gypsy! *Un poco dinero* will tickle the Gypsy's palm and give her visions! [*Straightens with a huge laugh, clapping his stomach.*]

PLAYER: On the Camino Real!

PROPRIETOR: Yes, on the Camino Real! Ha-ha-ha!

BLOCK IV

Jacques and Marguerite come out of hotel. She wears white with heaps of pale violets on her hat. They sit at the small round table which bears a sliced papaya and grapes and a tall green bottle and two rose-colored thin-stemmed glasses. A weird piping approaches. Proprietor returns outside to listen. Jacques rises nervously.

JACQUES: Mr. Gutman, we didn't ask for music!

MARGUERITE [*gently*]: Be still, Jacques. You know what it is.

PROPRIETOR: I'm sorry but there isn't much we can do about it. An Indian died of thirst today in the plaza. You see, the springs are dried up and there isn't a drop of water in the fountain and not everybody can afford to buy wine.

JACQUES: Doesn't the government do anything about it?

PROPRIETOR [*vaguely*]: Ah, the government! [*Fans himself with a palm leaf fan.*]

JACQUES: What kind of government is it?

PROPRIETOR: Democratic.

JACQUES: Well, I suspect it is really just a big corporation in which a few are stockholders and all the rest—petty wage-slaves!

PROPRIETOR: Does that strike you, sir, as being at all unique?

JACQUES: I have never been in a country, nominally Democratic or anything else, where even the most underprivileged citizen would be permitted to die of thirst in front of an hotel overflowing with wine.

PROPRIETOR: Have you—*travelled*, Senor?

JACQUES: Very widely.

PROPRIETOR: Then I can only assume that you have never looked out of your hotel windows!

MARGUERITE: Be careful, Jacques! [*The street-cleaners enter through arch at top of alley and advance into plaza, trundling their big white barrel on wheels, old German prints of the "Dance of Death" will suggest their appearance, except that they wear white jackets and caps and have brooms. They go to the fountain and kick the prostrate figure over on its back, pick it up and thrust it doubled up in the barrel. Then they lean on their brooms, whispering and giggling and staring at the couple.*] Waiter! [*He approaches. Marguerite, removing a bill from her purse.*] Give this to the men by the fountain and ask them to please move away. [*Waiter backs away fearfully.*]

PROPRIETOR: It's no use, Madam. Those two are the only public servants in town that are not susceptible to bribes. But don't look at them, only look at each other, and congratulate yourself on having your residence at the Siete Mares. Tonight there will be a fiesta!

MARGUERITE [*returning bill to her purse*]: What kind of fiesta?

PROPRIETOR: Whenever there's a full moon, the virginity of the Gypsy's daughter is publicly restored. She dances on the roof and her kinsmen dance in the plaza. It's the main attraction of our tourist season! Do you dance, Senor?

MARGUERITE: Senor Casanova has danced in all the courts of Europe.

PROPRIETOR: If he dances well enough to please the Gypsy's daughter, he might be invited inside—to lift her veil! Ha-ha! But I don't know—it's a doubtful honor! They tell me her mother turns a black card up for the chosen hero! [*Starts inside, laughing.*] Waiter! Bring the lady and gentleman a bottle of Lachrymae Christi with my compliments! And you—player of the blue guitar—*avante*! [*The lady turns full to the audience and her speech is delivered as a recitative with guitar accompaniment. The player stands close beside her and delicately keys his playing to her speech.*]

MARGUERITE: This dusty plaza with its dried-up fountain is like the skeleton of a scene from my youth. In a town of Provence where I once stayed for a summer there was a public fountain where the adolescent boys used to loiter at night. I had a precocious eye for them, at fifteen. It made a difference to me if they were slender and heavier in the shoulders than at the waist. I liked the gleam of white teeth and the attar of roses that some of them oiled their hair with. On a certain night of the week, I believe it was Thursday, it was customary for pairs of girls to walk around the fountain in one direction and pairs of boys in the other, and for the boys to offer bouquets of flowers to girls they wanted to call on. But the boy whose flowers I wanted did not take part in the walking about the fountain. He sat by the edge of the fountain and watched and smiled and the teeth in the Romany darkness of his face, for his father had been a gypsy, shone like a piece cut out of his starched white shirt. His eyes were northern, however, and startlingly blue. But he didn't return my look nor offer me flowers. And when the others had drifted away from the plaza, he still sat there. But then he picked up his guitar, and began to play! [*Bring guitar music up: Estrellita. The lady pushes her wine glass toward the bottle with a smile.*]

JACQUES: What is the point of this story?

MARGUERITE: You mean the moral? *Quien sabe!* [*Laughs.*] But wait till it's finished. . . . One summer evening, during the promenade—when I had been offered five or six bunches of flowers and turned them all down, all down!—I suddenly grabbed a bouquet that my friend had accepted . . .

JACQUES: Si?

MARGUERITE: And crossed to the fountain with my heart in my mouth. I went to where he was sitting, the handsome Gitano.—For you, I whispered!—I tossed the flowers toward him . . .

JACQUES: And then?

MARGUERITE: And then I ran home.

JACQUES: Did he call on you?

MARGUERITE: No.

JACQUES: So you languished away?

MARGUERITE: No, indeed.

JACQUES: So what did you do?

MARGUERITE: I learned of a path that he took going home late at night when the cantinas had closed.

JACQUES: Ha-ha!

MARGUERITE: I lay in wait for him there. I had a white dress on, I think he must have taken me for a ghost. He crossed himself and whispered the name of God's Mother!—But then I moaned and he knew—that I was—mortal. . . .

JACQUES: Ha-ha-ha!

MARGUERITE [*leaning back exultantly*]: That was the night that was talked about in the poem, the one that says that "The stars threw down their spears and watered heaven with their ears!"

JACQUES: They wept with pity because he passed you by?

MARGUERITE: They wept with joy because he—stopped—beside me. . . . [*Music: Tango. A pair of masked dancers enter the plaza, perform a brief, dramatic dance. Marguerite, as the dancers retire.*] I have had many loves. [*She drinks.*] But the time which I didn't dare think of, when youth would be lost, is now here. Yes, it's here and I'm here—sitting with someone for whom I have no desire—who has none for me—waiting to watch a young Gypsy dance on a roof—and trying to seem to ignore the ancient street-cleaners' impertinent glances at us! [*She touches his hand.*]

JACQUES [*ironically*]: Thank you.

MARGUERITE: We're used to each other. Yes, we've grown used to each other, and that's what passes for love at this far, moonlit end of the Camino Real.

JACQUES: The sort of violets—that can grow on the moon?

MARGUERITE: Or in the crevices of those far-away mountains, among the crevices—fertilized by the droppings of carrion-birds. . . . We're used to each other . . .

JACQUES: And when the street-cleaners approach us, and refuse to be bribed or distracted—when it's unmistakably plain that one of us or the other is being called for——Couldn't we—both——?

MARGUERITE: Go together?

JACQUES: Yes.

MARGUERITE: I don't know. I'm afraid to guess, Jacques. When you've spent as much of your heart as I've spent of mine, it's hard to conjecture how much of it may be left. [*Waiter brings wire to gentleman. He reads it and drops his head in his hands.*] What is it?

JACQUES: My remittances are cut off.

MARGUERITE: Completely?

[*Cancion: Minor Farolito.*]

JACQUES: Yes. [*Marguerite rises.*] Where are you going?

MARGUERITE [*carefully*]: I'm going to get a shawl. The evening comes so quickly and so cold. I can't afford to be chilled.

JACQUES [*springing up*]: Marguerite! [*Marguerite murmurs something indistinguishable. She enters hotel quickly. The street-cleaners giggle. Woman resumes song, "Farolito." He slumps back into his seat. The proprietor comes out.*]

PROPRIETOR: I hope you enjoyed your supper.

JACQUES: Yes, thank you.

PROPRIETOR: Oh, by the way, we are having to move you out of your room tonight. There was a mix-up in our reservations.

JACQUES: —Where can I go?

PROPRIETOR: You might try the Casa de Huespedes.

JACQUES: Where?

PROPRIETOR: It's across from the Laboratory. And your luggage is in the lobby. [*Goes back in. Jacques slowly follows. Now the guitar player indicates a division of scenes.*]

BLOCK V

Kilroy comes out of the pawn-shop. A lighter music. A foppish elderly man comes out of the cantina. He has on a light suit with a carnation in the lapel. Kilroy starts towards him. Notices the street-cleaners. Snatches up a rock and flings it at them. They

*dodge the missile and laugh. Skirting them widely, Kilroy crosses
to the elegant old man.*

KILROY: —Hey, Mac! It's wonderful to see you!

BARON: Really? Why?

KILROY: A normal American in a clean white suit!

BARON: My suit is pale yellow, my nationality is French and I am
not at all normal—but thanks! Can you give me the time?

KILROY: Nope. My watch is in a pawnshop on South Rampart
Street in New Orleans.

BARON: How about a light?

KILROY: I don't smoke.

BARON: You don't have any of the minor vices?

KILROY: I'm strictly a square. But you could do me a favor.

BARON: I'd be charmed to. What is it?

KILROY: Lend me five bucks on my belt!

BARON: Sorry.

KILROY: It's ruby and emerald studded!

BARON: It isn't my sort of thing. But if you should happen to find
the time or a light, ask for the Baron de Charlus at the desk. [*Baron
enters hotel: the proprietor chuckles. Kilroy crosses to him.*]

KILROY: —Could you——?

PROPRIETOR: There's an establishment across the Plaza where loans
can be secured on certain collateral.

KILROY: I've just been to the Loan Shark's. All he wanted was my
lucky gloves, which I'm not ready to part with.

PROPRIETOR: Better hold on to anything that's lucky, for little com-
punction is shown to a man without luck along here on the Camino
Real.

KILROY: What is the Camino Real?

PROPRIETOR: Everyone has to find that out for himself.

KILROY: Isn't there some way out?

PROPRIETOR: You see that narrow alley that goes by the Gypsy's and passes underneath the crumbling arch? That's The Way Out.

KILROY: I don't like the looks of it.

PROPRIETOR: Neither do I.

KILROY: There's mountains beyond it.

PROPRIETOR: Those mountains are covered with snow.

KILROY: A pair of skis would be useful.

PROPRIETOR [laughs]: Very! Ha-ha-ha! [The street-cleaners point and giggle.] I'm afraid you've attracted the attention of the street-cleaning department.

KILROY: What do they do with stiffs picked up in this town?

PROPRIETOR: It's better to have five dollars in your pocket. Otherwise you're removed to the laboratory.

KILROY: What happens there?

PROPRIETOR: You're taken apart. Your vital organs are put in pickle jars! [Laughs and enters hotel.]

KILROY: That's no way to treat a human body! [Jacques comes out with his luggage.] Hey, Mac!—As one gringo to another, in this mysterious place whose name isn't mentioned—could you——?

JACQUES: No, I couldn't. My remittances are cut off, I have just been evicted from the Siete Mares and abandoned by my last friend.

KILROY: Our situations are kind of embarrassing, ain't they? [Grins and extends his hand.] I'll see you later! [Starts across plaza.]—Buddy! [He kicks a rock thoughtfully. Jacques moves over. Kilroy slowly crosses the plaza toward the Loan Shark's, kicking a rock before him, and thoughtfully removing the golden gloves from about his neck. At a motion from the guitar player, the street-cleaners withdraw.]

[Cancion: "Neche de Ronda."]

BLOCK VI

PLAYER: *Ole!* The moon! [*The light changes as the full moon rises above the mountain range. A cool white radiance gilds the plaza. The woman sings at a distance, as Indians in dark blankets enter the plaza with lanterns and baskets covered with snowy clothes.*] Hoy! Noche de fiesta! [*The light falls on the roof of the Gypsy's. On it suddenly appears the Gypsy's daughter. She throws up her jewelled arms in a harsh flamenco cry. One of the Indians throws aside his blanket revealing a brilliant gypsy costume. He begins to dance. Then another. It is repeated till all the crowd is dancing. On the roof above them the Gypsy's daughter utters the sharp cries of the flamenco. The music changes. The Gypsy's daughter begins to dance on the roof, the others falling back to watch—except the player of the blue guitar who stands directly beneath her. Kilroy comes out of pawnshop, he is drawn across the plaza by her dancing. The crowd divides before him. He comes directly beneath the dancing girl. She looks down at him and stops moving except for her castanets.*] Ole! The Champion of the Golden Gloves! [*He begins to dance, first with rigid movements, then more freely, then with abandon. The girl utters the flamenco cries as he dances. At the climax of his dance the girl leans over the edge of the roof and tosses her flower to him. There is a great cry from the gathering.*] Ole! The Chosen Hero! [*Kilroy collapses with exhaustion. The male dancers seize him and lift him to their shoulders. There is a burst of fireworks. Roman candles on the roof of the Gypsy, pinwheels about the plaza, triumphal band music. The dancers form a parade, bearing Kilroy on their shoulders about the fountain while the girls pelt him with blossoms. He is borne to the door of the Gypsy's establishment and there set down on his feet. Kilroy is abashed and a little frightened. He gives the crowd an awkward salute, hoping they will disperse so he can slip quietly away. But they repeat their cheer and crowd closer about him. The door of the Gypsy's opens and a harsh female voice calls out: "PASE USTED!" The crowd echoes: "Pase Usted!" Seeing no way out, Kilroy hitches up his belt and slowly advances to the door. He salutes once more, then hesitantly enters: the door slams shut. The loudspeaker on the roof croaks continually like a cracked record: "That's all, that's all, that's all, that's all . . ." Voice: "Esmeralda, turn that damned thing off!" The loudspeaker squawks, then is silent. The crowd pick up their hats and rebozos and disperse singing in pairs. The plaza is empty except for Jacques and the flower-vendor. Jacques trails about the plaza, calling faintly:*]

JACQUES: Marguerite? Marguerite?

MADRECITA: Flores, flores para los muertos. Corones, corones para los muertos . . .

DIM OUT PLAZA

BLOCK VII

NOTE: *In this scene I am trying to catch the quality of really "tough" Americana of the comic sheets, the skid-row bars, cat-houses, Grade B movies, street-Arabs, vagrants, drunks, pitch-men, gamblers, whores, all the rootless, unstable and highly spirited life beneath the middle-class social level in the States. Lights up behind scrim at Gypsy's. This scene is one of Oriental or Moorish opulence as it might be dreamed of by a traveling salesman or drawn by Rube Goldberg, huge tasseled silk pillows, elaborate lamps, incense burners, occult signs and devices and chart of the heavens. There is a low table bearing an illuminated crystal ball. In the back is an alcove curtained off by sheer material. The Gypsy is discovered at a low round table which is covered with a cloth of purple silk, hanging to the floor with fringes of gold braid. On this table is the crystal ball and the deck of cards. She is peering into the crystal with jeweled fingers clasped to her temples. Kilroy enters through a curtain of beaded strings hanging to the left of the Gypsy. She appears to ignore his presence. He coughs to attract her attention.*

GYPSY: Siente se, por favor.

KILROY: No comprendo the lingo.

GYPSY: Yankee?

KILROY: Yankee.

GYPSY [*calling to rear*]: Yankee!

VOICE [*behind*]: Yankee! [*Kilroy laughs uneasily, wiping his brow with bandanna.*]

133

GYPSY: Name?

KILROY: Kilroy.

GYPSY: Address?

KILROY: Traveller.

GYPSY: Parents?

KILROY: I was brought up by an eccentric old aunt in Toledo.

GYPSY: Childhood diseases?

KILROY: Whooping cough, measles and mumps.

GYPSY [handing him a blank]: Sign this.

KILROY: What is it?

GYPSY: Just some kind of a blank. You always sign something, don't you?

KILROY: Not till I know what it is.

GYPSY: It's just a little formality to give a tone to the establishment and make an impression on our out-of-town trade. Roll up your sleeve.

KILROY: What for?

GYPSY: A shot of some kind.

KILROY: What kind?

GYPSY: Any kind. Don't they always give you some kind of a shot?

KILROY: "They?"

GYPSY: Brass-hats, Americanos! [Injects hypo.]

KILROY: I am no guinea pig!

GYPSY: Don't kid yourself. We're all of us guinea-pigs in the laboratory of God. Humanity is just a work in progress.

KILROY: I don't make it out.

GYPSY: Who does? The Camino Real is a funny paper read backwards, only we don't dare think about it much. [Weird piping outside.

Kilroy shifts nervously on his seat. Gypsy, grinning.] Tired? The altitude makes you sleepy?

KILROY: It makes me nervous.

GYPSY: I'll show you how to take a slug of tequila!—First you sprinkle salt on the back of your hand. Then lick it off with your tongue. Now then you toss the shot down! [*Demonstrates.*]—And then you bite into the lemon. That way it goes down easy, but what a bang!—You're next.

KILROY: No, thanks, I'm on the wagon.

GYPSY: There's an old Chinese proverb that says, "When your goose is cooked you might as well have it cooked with plenty of gravy." [*She laughs unpleasantly.*]—You're not a bad-looking boy. [*Puts on her glasses and moves around the table.*] Sometimes working for the Yankee dollar isn't a painful profession. Have you ever been attracted by older women?

KILROY: Frankly, no, ma'am.

GYPSY: Well, there's a first time for everything.

KILROY [*retreating awkwardly*]: That is a subject I cannot agree with you on.

GYPSY: You think I'm an old bag? [*Kilroy laughs awkwardly and moves behind table.*] Why are you crossing upstage? Ha-ha-ha! I am just the motherly type. Ain't that right, Esmeralda?

VOICE [*behind*]: *Si, Mama!*

GYPSY: Will you take the cards or the crystal?

KILROY: It's—immaterial.

GYPSY: All right, we'll begin with the cards. [*Shuffles and deals.*] Ask me a question.

KILROY: Has my luck run out?

GYPSY: Baby, your luck ran out the day you were born. Another question.

KILROY: Ought I to leave this town?

GYPSY: It don't look to me like you've got much choice in the matter. Take a card. [*Kilroy takes one.*] Ace?

KILROY: Yes, ma'am.

GYPSY: What color?

KILROY: Black.

GYPSY: That does it. How big is your heart?

KILROY: As big as the head of a baby.

GYPSY: It's going to break.

KILROY: That's what I was afraid of.

GYPSY: The street-cleaners are waiting for you outside the door.

KILROY: Which door, the front one? I'll slip out back!

GYPSY: It ain't no use. Leave us face it frankly, your number is up. [*Kilroy sinks back down thoughtfully. Street-cleaners' piping.*]

KILROY: I kind of figured as much. I've had a run of bad luck on the Camino Real. Sometimes you figure your luck is going to quit when you're too lucky and sometimes when luck ain't with you, you figure it's due. But when I landed here I had a feeling that this was the spot marked X on the chart of my life, and that X was not the spot where the treasure was buried. . . .

GYPSY: I like your good sense. You must've known a long time that the name of Kilroy was on the street-cleaners' list.

KILROY: Sure. But not on top of it!

GYPSY: Ha-ha-ha. It's always a bit of a shock. But here's good news. The Queen of Hearts has turned up in the proper position.

KILROY: What's that mean?

GYPSY: Love, Baby!

KILROY: Love?

GYPSY: Uh-huh. The Booby Prize!—Esmeralda! [*She rises and hits a gong.*] My daughter, Esmeralda! [*A light goes on in the alcove, making the diaphanous drapes transparent. The scene behind them is like a picture on the lid of a cigar box. The Gypsy's daughter is seated in a reclining position on a low divan of exotic shape and color. This is the little lady that danced on the roof. She is dressed in a gorgeous minimum of a costume. A spangled veil covers her face and it depends from a silver star on her forehead. From this veil to the girdle, below her navel, that supports her diaphanous bifurcated skirt, she is naked except for a pair of glittering emerald snakes upon her breasts.*]

KILROY [*after an appreciative glance*]: What's *her* specialty? *Tea leaves?*

GYPSY: Ha-ha!—Where is my pistol? I have to go out on the street!

ESMERALDA: You put it in the lower left-hand table drawer, Mama.

GYPSY: Good! I'm going to Walgreen's for change.

KILROY: What change?

GYPSY: The change from that ten-spot you are about to give me. [*Snaps her fingers. He slowly removes a bill.*]

KILROY: How'd you know I had it?

GYPSY: Oh, a little bird told me! [*Winks.*]

KILROY: I hocked my golden gloves to get this saw-buck, so don't go to Hollywood on it.

GYPSY: No one is gypped at the Gypsy's.—Such changeable weather! I'll slip on my summer furs! [*She throws on a greasy blanket and crosses to beaded string curtains.*] Adios! [*She is hardly offstage when two shots ring out.*]

ESMERALDA [*plaintively*]: Mother has such an awful time on the street. . . .

KILROY: You mean that she is insulted on the street?

ESMERALDA: Yes, by strangers.

KILROY: Well—I shouldn't think *acquaintances* would do it. [*Esmeralda curls up on the low divan in the alcove. There is a slight pause in which they regard each other.*]

137

KILROY [*hesitantly*]: Do you—do you like pictures? [*Esmeralda smiles and blinks rapidly.*] Here is a snapshot of my real true woman! [*Removes thumbed snapshot from wallet and extends to Esmeralda. She takes it with affected interest and stares at it with artificial smile. Kilroy, sadly.*] You're looking at it upside down. [*Esmeralda sighs and returns it to him.*] She was a platinum blonde the same as Jean Harlow. Do you remember Jean Harlow? [*Esmeralda shakes head.*] No, you wouldn't remember Jean Harlow. It shows you are getting old when you remember Jean Harlow. [*Puts snapshot away.*] . . . They say that Jean Harlow's ashes are kept in a little private cathedral at Forest Lawn. . . . Wouldn't it be wonderful if you could sprinkle them ashes over the ground like seeds, and out of each one would spring another Jean Harlow? And when spring comes you could just walk out and pick them off the bush! [*He grins enthusiastically but Esmeralda yawns, touching her lips delicately with a tiny handkerchief.*] You don't talk much.

ESMERALDA: You want me to talk?

KILROY: Well, that's the way we do things in the States. A little vino, some records on the victrola, some quiet conversation—and then if both parties are in a mood for romance . . . [*Gesture.*]

ESMERALDA: Oh. . . . [*She rises indolently and pours some wine from a slender crystal decanter. Starts victrola playing softly. "Quiereme Mucho." Returns to divan and strikes a voluptuous pose. Watching her movements, Kilroy's mouth sags open and waters—he wipes it with bandanna. After a thoughtful pause.*] They say that the monetary system has got to be stabilized all over the world.

KILROY [*taking glass*]: Huh?

ESMERALDA: It has to do with some kind of agreement which was made in the woods.

KILROY: Oh.

ESMERALDA: How do you feel about the class-struggle? Do you take sides in that?

KILROY: No.

ESMERALDA: Neither do we, because of the dialectics.

KILROY: The which?

ESMERALDA: Languages with accents, I suppose. But all we hope is that they will not bring the Pope over here and put him in the White House.

KILROY: Who?

ESMERALDA: Oh, the Bolsheviskies, those nasty old things with whiskers. And how do you feel about the Mumbo Jumbo? Do you think they've gotten the Old Man in the bag yet?

KILROY: The Old Man?

ESMERALDA: God. We don't think so. We think there has been so much of the Mumbo Jumbo it's put Him to sleep. [*Giggles.*] What are you thinking about?

KILROY: Those green snakes over your——What do you wear them for?

ESMERALDA: Oh, so that's what you're really interested in!—Never mind the class-struggle. The stabilization can go and jump in a lake! And what do you care if the Old Man likes the Mumbo Jumbo or not! Your question is, why do I wear the green snakes over my breasts! [*Delicately.*] Ha-ha!—Well, I will tell you! Supposedly for protection—but, really, for fun! [*Kilroy gets up slowly.*] What are you going to do?

KILROY: I'm about to establish a beach-head on that sofa. [*Esmer alda giggles and moves coyly aside, patting the space beside her. Kilroy, sitting down gingerly.*] How about—lifting your veil?

ESMERALDA [*looking shyly down*]: I can't lift it.

KILROY: Why not?

ESMERALDA: I promised Mother I wouldn't.

KILROY: I thought your mother was the broadminded type.

ESMERALDA: Oh, she is, but you know how mothers are. [*Then impulsively.*] If you say pretty please you can lift it for me!

KILROY: Awww——

ESMERALDA: Go on, say it! Say pretty please!

KILROY: No!!

ESMERALDA: Why not?

KILROY: It's silly!

ESMERALDA: Then you can't lift my veil!

KILROY: Oh, all right. Pretty please.

ESMERALDA: Say it again!

KILROY: Pretty please.

ESMERALDA: Now say it once more like you meant it! [*He jumps up. She grabs his hand.*] Don't go away.

KILROY: You're making a fool out of me.

ESMERALDA: I was just teasing a little. Because you're so cute. Sit down again, please—*pretty* please! [*He sits back down.*]

KILROY: What is that wonderful perfume you've got on?

ESMERALDA: Guess!

KILROY: Chanel Number Five?

ESMERALDA: No.

KILROY: Tabu?

ESMERALDA: No.

KILROY: I give up.

ESMERALDA: It's *Noche en Acapulco!* [*Then, plaintively.*] I'm just dying to go to Acapulco. [*She places her forefinger against his chest and wriggles coyly.*] I wish that you would take me to Acapulco.

KILROY [*groaning*]: It's always like this.

ESMERALDA: What?

KILROY: You Gypsys' daughters are invariably reminded of something without which you cannot do—just when it looks like everything has been fixed!

ESMERALDA: That isn't nice at all. I'm not the gold-digger type. Some girls see themselves in silver foxes. I only see myself in Acapulco!

KILROY: At Todd's place?

ESMERALDA: Oh, no, at the Mirador! Watching those pretty boys dive off the Quebrada!

KILROY: Look again, Baby. Maybe you'll see yourself in Paramount Pictures or having a Singapore Sling at a Statler bar!

ESMERALDA: You're being sarcastic?

KILROY: Nope. Just realistic. Excuse me while I go home. [*She grabs his hand again and purrs like a cat.*]

ESMERALDA: Your hand is cold!

KILROY: The romance is gone and the glamor is dissipated.

ESMERALDA: Ohhhh—*Pobracita!* [*She kisses his fingers.*]

KILROY: All of you Gypsys' daughters have hearts of stone, and I'm not whistling Dixie! But just the same, the night before a man dies, he says, "Pretty please—will you let me lift your veil?"—while the street-cleaners wait for him right outside the door!—Because to be warm for a little longer is life. And love?—That's a four-letter word which is sometimes no better than one you see printed on fences by kids playing hooky from school!—Oh, well—what's the use of complaining? You Gypsys' daughters have ears that only catch sounds like the snap of a gold cigarette case! Or, pretty please, Baby—we're going to Acapulco!

ESMERALDA: *Are* we?

KILROY: Yes! In the morning!

ESMERALDA: Ohhhh! [*She moves her head in a weaving motion.*] I'm dizzy with joy! My little heart is going pitty-pat!

KILROY: My big heart is going boom-boom! Can I lift your veil now?

ESMERALDA: If you will be gentle.

KILROY: I would not hurt a fly unless it had on leather mittens. [*He touches a corner of her spangled veil. She moans.*]

ESMERALDA: Ohhhh . . .

KILROY: What?

ESMERALDA [*louder*]: *Ohhhh!*

KILROY: Why! What's the matter?

ESMERALDA: You are not being gentle!

KILROY: I *am* being gentle.

ESMERALDA: You are *not* being gentle.

KILROY: What was I being, then?

ESMERALDA: Rough!

KILROY: I am not being rough.

ESMERALDA: Yes, you *are* being rough. You have to be gentle with me because you're the first.

KILROY: Are you kidding?

ESMERALDA: No.

KILROY: How about all of those other fiestas you've been to?

ESMERALDA: Each one's the first one. That is the wonderful thing about Gypsys' daughters!

KILROY: You can say that again!

ESMERALDA: I don't like you when you're like that.

KILROY: Like what?

ESMERALDA: Cynical and sarcastic.

KILROY: I am sincere.

ESMERALDA: Lots of boys aren't sincere.

KILROY: Maybe they aren't but I am.

ESMERALDA: Everyone says he's sincere, but everyone isn't sincere. If everyone was sincere who says he's sincere there wouldn't be half so many insincere ones in the world and there would be lots, lots, lots more really sincere ones!

KILROY: I think you have got something there. But how about Gypsys' daughters?

ESMERALDA: Huh?

KILROY: Are they one hundred percent in the really sincere category?

ESMERALDA: Well, yes, and no, mostly no! But some of them are for a while if their sweethearts are gentle.

KILROY: Would you believe that I am sincere and gentle?

ESMERALDA: I would believe that you believe that you are. [*Pause.*] For a while. . . .

KILROY: Everything's for a while. For a while is the stuff that dreams are made of, Baby! [*Music under.*] Now?—*Now?*

ESMERALDA: Yes, now, but be gentle!—*gentle.* . . . [*He delicately lifts a corner of her veil. She utters a soft cry. He lifts it further. She cries out again. A bit further. She presses a hand to his chest and leans her head back almost out of his reach. Then with a low moan he seizes her head and draws it forcibly toward him while he slowly and deliberately turns the spangled veil all the way up from her face. Her face, revealed for the first time, is drawn into a look of oblivious and ecstatic pain. Softly, with closed eyes.*] I am sincere, I am sincere, I am sincere!

[*Rapturous harp music.*]

KILROY: I am sincere, I am sincere, I am sincere! [*The music dies out. Kilroy leans back in an attitude of exhaustion, removing his hand from her veil. She slowly opens her eyes and looks at him with troubled wonder.*]

ESMERALDA: Is that all?

KILROY: I am tired.

ESMERALDA: Already? [*She rises slowly and goes wearily down the three steps from the alcove. He speaks with his back to her.*]

KILROY: I am tired, and full of regret. . . .

ESMERALDA [*her face hardening*]: —Oh . . .

KILROY: It wasn't much to give my golden gloves for!

ESMERALDA: You pity yourself?

KILROY: That's right, I pity myself and everybody that goes to the Gypsy's daughter. I pity the world and I pity the God who made it. [*Sits down with his back to her.*]

[*Sad music.*]

ESMERALDA: It's always like that as soon as the veil is lifted. They're all so ashamed of having degraded themselves, and their hearts have more regret than a heart can hold!

KILROY [*bowing his head to his hands*]: Even a heart that's as big as the head of a baby!

ESMERALDA: You don't even notice how pretty my face is, do you?

KILROY: You look like all Gypsys' daughters, no better, no worse. But as long as you get to go to Acapulco, your cup runneth over with ordinary contentment.

ESMERALDA: —I've never been so insulted in all my life!

[*Music out.*]

KILROY: Oh, yes, you have, Baby. And you'll be insulted worse if you stay in this racket. You'll be insulted so much that it will get to be like water off a duck's back! [*Door slams. The beaded curtains are drawn apart on the Gypsy. Esmeralda lowers her veil hastily and turns her back to them. Kilroy pretends not to notice the Gypsy's entrance. She picks up a little bell and rings it over his head.*] Okay, Mamacita! I am aware of your presence!

GYPSY: Ha-ha! I was followed three blocks by some awful man!

KILROY: Did you catch him? [*She gives him a playful shove.*]

GYPSY: He ducked into a subway! I waited fifteen minutes outside the men's room and he never came out!

KILROY: Then you went in?

GYPSY: No! I met a sailor!—The streets are brilliant! [*Throwing up both hands.*] Have you all been good children? [*Esmeralda makes a whimpering sound. Gypsy, knowingly.*] Ohhhh! The pussy will play while the old mother cat is away? [*Kilroy gets up, hitching his belt.*]

KILROY: Your sense of humor is wonderful, but how about my change, Mamacita!

GYPSY: What change are you talking about?

KILROY, Are you boxed out of your mind? The change from that ten-spot you trotted over to Walgreen's?

GYPSY: Ohhhh——

KILROY: Oh, *what?*

GYPSY [*counting on her jewelled fingers*]: Five for the works, one dollar luxury tax, two for the house percentage and two more *pour la service!*—makes *ten!* Didn't I tell you?

KILROY: —What kind of a deal is this?

GYPSY [*whipping out her little pearl-handled revolver*]: A rugged one, Baby!

ESMERALDA: Mama, don't be unkind!

GYPSY: Honey, the gentleman's friends are waiting outside and it wouldn't be nice to detain him!

KILROY [*slowly*]: Okay, Mamacita! Me voy! [*He crosses to the beaded string curtains. Turns and looks back, at the Gypsy and Esmeralda. The weird piping of the street-cleaners is heard outside. Esmeralda twists a ring on her finger. The Gypsy polishes her fingernails with elaborate unconcern.*]—Sincere?—Sure! Completely!—That's the wonderful thing about Gypsys' daughters! [*He goes out. Esmeralda raises a wondering fingertip to one eye. Then cries out in a tone of joyous surprise.*]

ESMERALDA: Look, Mama! Look, Mama! A *tear!* [*The light fades out on the phoney paradise of the Gypsy's. The transparency descends. The light returns to the street.*]

BLOCK VIII

There are three figures in the moonlit plaza as Kilroy emerges from the Gypsy's. The player of the blue guitar, standing by the fountain, La Madrecita, by the foot of the alley, Jacques Casanova at the table before the hotel. He has a glass and a wine bottle. This third area is lighted most. Kilroy descends into the plaza with the manner of scared child entering a dark room.

MADRECITA [*lifting her flowers*]: Flores, flores para los muertos, corones, corones para los muertos?

KILROY: No hay dinero. [*Slips past her, glancing nervously about. Sees the gentleman at the table. Starts toward him. With attempted heartiness that rings flat.*] Hey, Mac! [*Jacques looks up slowly.*] How is your situation? Has it improved?

JACQUES: It has deteriorated to a point at which it is only possible to improve.

KILROY: Ha-ha! That's the way to look at it!

JACQUES: Have a seat. Did you enjoy the fiesta?

KILROY: It was a little more than I bargained for, Mac.

JACQUES: How so?

KILROY: I got mixed up with the daughter of the Gypsy. They seem to be running a sort of high-class clip-joint over there.

JACQUES: Did the ladies impose on your trusting nature?

KILROY: You can say that twice, and still repeat it! [*Piping.*] Have you—uh—seen the street-cleaners—lately?

JACQUES: Not since supper, thank God! Are you expecting them?

KILROY: The Gypsy told me that I was on top of their list.

JACQUES: I can't be very far down on it myself.

KILROY: Maybe our numbers have come up together.

JACQUES: As much as I appreciate your company, sir—I cannot regard that as a happy thought.

KILROY: Then skip it.

JACQUES: I will try to. [*Piping again, somewhat closer.*] It's just wind, you know. The wind in the chimney.

KILROY: Sure!—What are you drinking?

JACQUES [*pushing bottle toward him*]: The dregs of a wasted life. The souvenirs of a gentleman of fortune who had talent and energy enough to have been a leader of multitudes but was only a lover of women.

KILROY: Is that so bad?

JACQUES: Not if you're a successful lover, but a successful lover is relatively faithful.

KILROY: And you cheated? [*A minor waltz fades in.*]

JACQUES: I was a wolf. To be a wolf is to be the victim of an emotional impotence, and I have been one of the most insatiable wolves on record. I have scrambled from one bed-chamber to another with shirt-tails always on fire, from girl to girl, like buckets of coal-oil poured on a conflagration, down and down the precipitous alley of life, till I came here, where there's no girl and no bed—and this is my last wine-bottle, presented to me with the compliments of the hotel manager who has just thrown me out on my ear because my remittances are cut off and my lady has left me! The name of the wine is a joke. It is Lachrymae Christi which means the Tears of Christ. He might have wept for me once, but all He could give me now is a groan of disgust. [*Laughs and pours Kilroy some wine.*]

[*Music out.*]

KILROY: Thanks, Mac. I'm also a has-been. A former champion of the golden gloves. I also used to be a Casanova!

JACQUES: Ah?

KILROY: Do you like to look at pictures?

JACQUES: French ones?

KILROY: No, just girls.

JACQUES: Ah. . . . [*Kilroy takes out a collection of ragged snap-shots. The piping is heard considerably closer, shrill giggling, moan of wind.*]

KILROY [*touching his chest*]: Hear that?

JACQUES: I'm afraid I do, but let's pretend that we don't. Who is this young lady attired for bathing?

KILROY: A cookie I used to cut in San Antone.

JACQUES: Beautiful eyes! And this one?

KILROY: A seventeen-year-old Ginny I had in L. A.

JACQUES: Milk-fed chicken! This one?

KILROY: I shacked up with her at the Sherman Hotel in Chicago. [*Giggle and piping very close. Kilroy springs up. Kilroy hoarsely.*] That's them, the street-cleaners!

JACQUES: Sit down, sit down, Chicquito! Who are these nymphs?

KILROY [*very nervously*]: Betsy Lou and Martha Jane Thompkins, identical twins, in Omaha, Nebraska.

JACQUES: Who was lucky Piere?

KILROY: Ha-ha!—Here's my real true woman.

JACQUES: The prettiest of the lot!

KILROY: Yeah, she was my wife. I married her eight years ago, the night after I knocked out the Monterrey killer.

JACQUES: You lucky dog! I never had a wife. [*Piping. Kilroy starts up again. Casanova touches his shoulder. He sinks back nervously in his seat.*] Was she faithful to you?

KILROY: Sure she was.

JACQUES: But you grew tired of her?

KILROY: *Never!* It was for *her* sake I quit her. . . . [*Giggle, considerably closer.*] Yeh, *they're* coming!

JACQUES: *Shhh!* The excitement would always pass for me too quickly. They say it comes back again, if you're patient enough. And that's when the really wonderful part commences, when love is not just a rented room—but a home that you can rest in! Where you can unpack your books and hang your pictures! [*Kilroy has slumped in his chair a little.*] What is the matter?

KILROY: I have trouble—breathing. . . .

JACQUES: Don't be frightened!—Who is this young lady?

KILROY [*in painful gasps*]: That's—Vivian! I met her on Benefit Street—in Providence—Rhode Island. [*The piping is now continuous and quite near.*] Will you—hold my hand—please?

JACQUES [*softly*]: Going?

KILROY: *Si! Me Voy!* [*Casanova takes his hand and embraces his sagging shoulders.*]

JACQUES [*gently*]: Isn't it silly? We two old Casanovas, holding hands!

KILROY [*breathlessly*]: Ha-ha!

JACQUES: Like a pair of timid old maids at the sound of a mouse in the woodwork!

KILROY: Ha-ha!

JACQUES: Ha-ha-ha!

KILROY: Ha-ha-ha-ha! [*He suddenly pitches over and falls to the street. Street-cleaners enter through arch and advance down the alley. Jacques falls slowly back from the table and flattens himself against the wall of the Siete Mares as the frightful figures approach with their giggles and piping. They come up to Kilroy's fallen body. Search the pockets. They double him up and stuff him into the barrel. They start off. One of them notices Jacques and points.*]

STREET-CLEANER: *Buenos noces, Senor Casanova!* [*The other street-cleaner giggles mockingly. Jacques averts his face to the wall. They trundle their barrel off into left wings, where a sign points: "To the Laboratory."*]

LA MADRECITA: Flores, flores, para los muertos? Corones, corones para los muertos? [*Jacques returns slowly to the table and finds the wine bottle empty. The player of the guitar strikes a chord and the scene dims out except for a faint spot of light on La Madrecita with her gaudy tin flowers.*]

BLOCK IX

Two areas are spotted, one upstage at the foot of the Alley Way out. In this area is seated the old woman flower-vendor, and across her knees, in the attitude of Michelangelo's Pieta, is the body of Kilroy. The other lighted area is downstage center where a low white table on wheels bears a sheeted figure. Beside the table stands a medical instructor addressing a pair of students, all in white surgical jackets.

INSTRUCTOR: This is the body of an unidentified vagrant.

MADRECITA: This was thy son, America—and now mine.

INSTRUCTOR: He was found in an alley along the Camino Real.

MADRECITA: He had blue eyes and the body of a champion boxer.

INSTRUCTOR: There is no external evidence of disease. There are no marks of violence on the body.

MADRECITA: He had the soft voice of the South, and a pair of golden gloves—but the deal was rugged.

INSTRUCTOR: His death was apparently due to natural causes. [*Students make notes. Keening voices.*]

MADRECITA: Yes, blow wind where night thins! He had many loves, many loves. . . .

INSTRUCTOR: In the absence of legal claimants, no friends or relatives having identified him——

MADRECITA: He stood as a planet among the moons of their longing, haughty with youth, a champion of the prize-ring! You should have seen the lovely, monogrammed robe in which he strode the aisles of the Colisseums!

INSTRUCTOR: After elapse of a certain number of days, his body becomes the property of the State——

MADRECITA: Yes, blow wind where night thins—for laurel is not everlasting. . . .

INSTRUCTOR: And now is transferred to our hands for the nominal sum of five dollars.

MADRECITA: This was thy son, America—and now mine. . . .

INSTRUCTOR: We will now proceed with the dissection. Knife, please!

MADRECITA: Blow, wind! [*Sound of wind, keening voices.*] Yes, blow wind where night thins! You are his passing bell and his lamentation!

VOICES: Ay, ay, ay!

[*Student crosses to doctor with knife.*]

MADRECITA: Keen for him all maimed creatures, deformed and mutilated—his homeless ghost is your own!

INSTRUCTOR: First we will open up the chest cavity and examine the heart for evidence of coronary occlusion.

MADRECITA: His heart was pure gold and as big as the head of a baby.

INSTRUCTOR: We will make an incision along the vertical line.

[*Sound: wind.*]

MADRECITA [*touching Kilroy's forehead with her flowers*]: Rise, ghost! Go, bird! "Humankind cannot bear very much reality." [*At the touch of her flowers, Kilroy stirs and pushes himself slowly up from the lap of the madrecita. He rubs his eyes, then springs to his feet and looks around him.*]

VOICES: Ole! Ole! Ole! The chosen hero! [*The madrecita makes a gesture of benediction. She then turns and passes slowly up the alley.*]

KILROY: Hey! Hey, somebody! Where am I? [*He notices the lighted area of the dissection room and approaches slowly.*]

DOCTOR [*removing a glittering sphere from the dummy corpse*]: Look at this heart. It's as big as the head of a baby.

KILROY [*indignantly*]: My heart!?

DOCTOR: Put it in the basin and wash it off so we can look for the pathological lesions.

KILROY [*awestruck*]: Yes, siree, that's my heart! [*He pauses just outside the lighted area as a student takes the heart and dips it into a basin on stand beside table, suddenly cries out and holds aloft a glittering gold sphere.*]

STUDENT: Hey, Doc! This heart's solid gold! [*Drums, cymbals, other festive noises.*]

KILROY [*rushing forward*]: That's mine, you bastards! [*He snatches the gold heart from the student and dashes into right wings.*]

INSTRUCTOR: Stop, thief! Stop, corpse! [*They all pursue Kilroy offstage.*]

BLACKOUT

BLOCK X

Faint light before daybreak. Esmeralda appears on the Gypsy's roof, enveloped in a diaphanous scarf sprinkled with iridescent silver stars. She stands there like a somnambulist, eyes closed and lips slightly parted in a childish smile. Kilroy enters from right wings. Sees Esmeralda and whistles. She gives no sign of attention. The music of the fiesta scene is revived in a ghostly key, much softer, as if played at a distance. The Fiesta dancers enter. They are all in ghostly white costumes and their faces covered with neo-classic white masks. A spectral ballet is performed to the eerie music. Kilroy then performs a solo dance directly under the roof. Esmeralda remains with closed eyes. Finally he tosses his heart in the air to catch her attention, and calls her name.

KILROY: Hey! Esmeralda!

ESMERALDA [*without looking down*]: Go away, cat!

DANCERS [*mockingly*]: Ole! The Chosen Hero! [*They scatter from the stage with mocking laughter. Kilroy is momentarily baffled. Then a happy thought strikes him and be dashes over to the Loan Shark's and bangs at the door. It opens instantly and the interior lights up.*]

KILROY [*entering*]: Quanto por mi corazon? Un corazon de oro! [*The guitar player strolls out of the cantina playing the song Estrellita, followed by the woman singer. They cross to the Gypsy's and serenade Esmeralda. She dances dreamily on the roof. Kilroy comes back out laden with articles procured in exchange for his heart. A fur coat, a gown of sequins, ropes of pearls, a rhinestone tiara—a fistful of colored pasteboard tickets, a doll with golden curls and a bunch of balloons. He dashes over to point beneath where Esmeralda is standing.*] Hey! Esmeralda!

ESMERALDA [*without looking down*]: Go away, cat! Go away, cat!

KILROY: Look who's here! Me! Kilroy!

ESMERALDA: Go away, cat!

KILROY: Aw, don't be sore! I didn't mean to insult you! You misunderstood me, honey. Now look what I've got. Tickets to Acapulco and everywhere else! A real mink coat that was worn by Hedy LaMarr! Hey! Look! [*He releases the colored balloons. They float directly past her. She stretches out her arms.*]

ESMERALDA: Oh, how pretty! [*Then, sadly.*] They're gone. [*She turns and disappears from the roof. Kilroy drops his presents on the street and rushes up to the Gypsy's door and bangs with both fists. The door is thrown open. A pail of water is thrown into his face.*]

GYPSY: *Scat!* [*The door slams shut. He backs down into the alley, gasping and spluttering.*]

KILROY [*in final disgust*]: How do you like them apples! [*A faint, weird music commences. It seems to come from the cantina. The swinging doors push open on a remarkable figure. It is a tall, lank figure dressed as a knight of chivalry, silver armor which is loose and rusty. But the plume on his helmet is downy and white as snow in the rosy light from the cantina's entrance. As he advances with stately, clanking stride, his face also catches the light. It is long and lean and weatherbeaten, and the very wide open eyes are immensely grave in the old and haunted red face. Kilroy, still facing the Gypsy's.*] The hell with all of you phoney Gypsys' daughters. [*The ancient knight stops near Kilroy. As the downcast youth turns toward him, the knight's face softens into a smile.*]

KNIGHT: *Que paso, mi amigo?*

KILROY: The deal is rugged! Do you know what I mean?

KNIGHT: Who knows better than I what a rugged deal is! But will you take some advice?

KILROY: I'll take anything at this point.

KNIGHT: *Don't—pity—your—self!* [*He touches Kilroy's chest with his long forefinger.*] Ha-ha! The wounds of the vanity, the many offenses our egos have to endure——Being housed in bodies that age, and hearts that grow tired—are better accepted with a tolerant smile—like this! Y'see? [*He stretches his weatherbeaten face into an enormous grin.*] Otherwise what you become is a bag full of curdled cream—*leche mala* we call it!—attractive to nobody, least of all to yourself.

KILROY: —*Who* are you?

KNIGHT: Quixote. Quixote de la Mancha!—Heard of me?

KILROY: Sort of—somewhere, I think.

KNIGHT: Have y' got any plans?

KILROY: No, sir.

KNIGHT: Then come along with me!

KILROY: *Donde?*

KNIGHT: *Quien sabe!*—Who cares!

KILROY [*after a slight reflection*]: *Como no*——[*Crosses to sign* "KILROY IS HERE," *scratches out* "IS" *and prints* "WAS."]

KNIGHT: Sancho!

SANCHO: Si, Senor! Si—Senor. . . .

KNIGHT: Ha-ha! *Vaminos!* [*They lock arms and start up the steep alley together. Bring light up on table before Siete Mares where Jacques is seated with his head in his arms. Marguerite appears at the other side of the plaza. She crosses to the table. He looks up slowly and slowly rises.*]

JACQUES: I thought you had left me forever.

MARGUERITE: I've only been looking at silver.

JACQUES: They've locked me out of my room.

MARGUERITE: It's all right. I'll take you to mine. Why, Jacques—you're crying! [*She sinks into chair. He crouches at her feet and buries his face in her lap. Marguerite, touching his head.*] The violets in the mountains are breaking the rocks!

KNIGHT [*at the top of the alley*]: Hey! Sancho! Sancho Panza!

[*They pause under the crumbling arch. Sancho Panza stumbles out of the cantina of the Siete Mares, rubber-legged and wobbling under a load of durious knightly equipment.*]

SANCHO: So, Senor! Si—Senor. . . .

QUIXOTE (KNIGHT) [*passionately*]: *Vaminos!*

SANCHO [*wearily*]: *Si, Senor. Me voy, Senor.—Me—voy* . . . [*He turns a bit dizzily. Then starts up the alley way out. The music rises tenderly and richly as the player of the blue guitar steps into the moonlit plaza. A woman sings at a distance. He looks about him. Then stretches his arms in a gesture of wonder and finality.*]

THE END

A PLAYWRIGHT WITH A
SOCIAL CONSCIENCE

In 1966, Tennessee Williams was asked by an interviewer if he would ever write "directly" about current political events including the struggle of African-Americans for civil rights and the Vietnam War. "I am not a direct writer," Williams replied, "I am always an oblique writer, if I can be; I want to be allusive; I don't want to be one of those people who hit the nail on the head all the time." This did not mean, however, that the important political and social events of his time had no interest for him. Nine years later, in the wake of Watergate, Nixon's resignation and—still—Vietnam, Williams said to another interviewer, "All my plays have a social conscience."

Both statements are true. His earliest plays were born out of the political and social temper—and the political and social drama—of their time. Like Clifford Odets and Irwin Shaw (whose plays for the politically-committed Group Theatre the young playwright knew), Williams in the mid-1930s found that he was best able to express his personal hopes and anxieties through the experiences of people he read about in newspapers: the coal miners of Alabama (*Candles to the Sun*), the homeless and dispossessed of St. Louis (*The Fugitive Kind*) and the inmates of a Pennsylvania penitentiary (*Not About Nightingales*). In later plays, politics and social struggle receded to the background. Or did they?

> In Spain there was revolution. Here there was only shouting and
> confusion. In Spain there was Guernica. Here there were distur-
> bances of labor, sometimes pretty violent, in otherwise peaceful
> cities such as Chicago, Cleveland, Saint Louis . . . This is the social
> background of the play.

Beyond a further poetic reference to the "adventure and change" that awaited Tom's generation "in the folds of Chamberlain's umbrella," there is little other mention of the larger world in *The Glass Menagerie*. Yet, all the characters in the play, perhaps excepting Laura, are influenced by the same desperation that affected so many of those who lived through those years. The Great Depression of the 1930s is, in fact, the most important given circumstance of the play: the Wingfields live in an apartment too small for them because they can't afford a larger one; Tom slaves in a shoe warehouse for a few dollars a week so that they can manage even that; Amanda makes plans and provisions to safeguard her children from the perils of a dangerous time. Is the outside world really in the background if it's in the front of everyone's daily thoughts?

The same is true of much of Williams's later work. *Camino Real* is one of Williams's most political plays, both in the circumstances of its creation and in its content, but the content doesn't consist of uncontradicted slogans or simple actions that climax in a clenched fist or a slaughter of the innocents. It is allusive and elusive.

As for its creation: In 1949, Elia Kazan began using scenes from Williams's one-act version of the play, called *Ten Blocks on the Camino Real*, as an exercise at the Actors Studio. Inspired by the results, Williams decided to expand the material into a full-length play. By the time he'd finished, Cold War fears of Communist infiltration of the government and the culture had set in. In March 1953, when *Camino Real* opened on Broadway, Senator Joseph McCarthy's Senate subcommittee on investigations was in full swing, as was the House Committee on Un-American Activities, known as HUAC, which had been attempting to ferret out Communists in the entertainment world off and on since the mid-1930s. In a panic over losing sponsors and audiences, television and film executives established blacklists of writers, actors and directors whose testimony before HUAC was not deemed sufficiently patriotic. Many lost their jobs, and a deep sense of fear enveloped the industry, reflecting a general paranoia in the country at large. The Gypsy's Act One announcement on her loudspeaker sums up the feeling:

> Are you afraid of anything at all? Afraid of your heartbeat? Or the
> eyes of strangers! Afraid of breathing? Afraid of not breathing? Do
> you wish that things could be straight and simple again as they were
> in your childhood? Would you like to go back to Kindy Garten?

In this atmosphere, Williams had to decide whether or not to stick by his choice of Elia Kazan to direct *Camino*. In 1952, Kazan was called to testify before HUAC. At first he wouldn't identify any of his former Group Theatre colleagues who, like him, had been members of the Communist Party in the 1930s. When the news broke, Williams wrote to his friend Maria St. Just that Kazan's refusal to give the Committee names was "very admirable of him, and very brave, and all decent people ought to respect his sense of honor about it. But of course most of them don't!" After Kazan ran a long ad in the *New York Times* defending his ultimate decision to name names, Williams wrote his agent, Audrey Wood, that the act was "a very sad comment on our Times [sic]." Still, he stood by Kazan, and the director was grateful that Williams proved loyal at a time when many of his friends turned their backs.

Williams's loyalty, however, had as much to do with self-interest as with political courage. He was acutely aware that his two previous plays, *Summer and Smoke* and *The Rose Tattoo* (Kazan had agreed to direct the latter and then changed his mind), had lost money, and he wanted the new play to be a financial success. Although he'd briefly considered other, younger directors such as Peter Brook and José Quintero, Williams decided that Kazan, who had directed both the Broadway and film versions of *A Streetcar Named Desire*, was the best insurance against another failure. In a subsequent letter to St. Just, Williams turned apolitical and expressed skepticism that Kazan would return his loyalty: "I take no attitude about [Kazan's testimony] one way or another, as I am not a political person and human venality is something I always expect and forgive. But I am not yet sure that Gadge will not disappoint me, personally, as he did with *Tattoo*."

Then there was the matter of Arthur Miller. A few months after *Camino*'s Broadway run ended, Williams wrote a letter of protest to the State Department for denying Miller a passport to travel to Europe to attend the Belgian premier of *The Crucible*. At the last minute, fearful that his own passport request would be denied, Williams didn't mail it. He wrote the *New York Times* critic Brooks Atkinson that his inaction, "shows what an atmosphere of intimidation has come to exist among us."

If Williams hesitated over Kazan and Miller, he was quite forthright in his handling of the Baron de Charlus. This character, borrowed from Proust, barely exists in the one-act *Camino* that Kazan worked on at the

Actors Studio. After seven unrevealing lines of dialogue, he disappears. Williams fleshed out this walk-on character for the full-length version. The result was still a minor role, but one that made a significant statement: At a time when gay men and women were also the targets of government-sponsored witch hunts (six weeks after *Camino* opened, President Eisenhower issued an executive order instructing heads of federal departments that "sexual perversion" was not only sufficient but necessary grounds for dismissal from government jobs), this character, created for a commercial production on Broadway, was a very gay and outré figure who is murdered by agents of the government for the crime of being different.

The desire to be circumspect, the decision to be bold, a willingness to overlook the larger political issue to focus on a personal one, are all reflected in the text of the play. The world of *Camino Real* is one of fear and of courageous personal gestures. The central conflict is between two forces. Power is represented by Gutman, his police officers and Street Cleaners (the two sinister, aptly named figures who, at the command of the state, kill and then sweep away the dreamers and troublemakers). Gutman and his associates deny the one remaining source of water on the Camino Real to the poor and dispossessed, and guard against the forbidden word—*Hermano*—being spoken in public, where it might lead to uprising and revolution. On the other side are the "legendary figures," the Romantic characters borrowed from history and literature who believe in what Williams called the "romantic attitude toward life," including Jacques Casanova, Marguerite Gautier, the Baron De Charlus, Lord Byron and a contemporary American, Kilroy. If Williams's purpose was to hit the political nail on the head, we would expect the Romantics to actively oppose Gutman and his forces of repression, to "search for a way to live romantically, with 'honor', in our times . . .", (as Williams described the play's theme at one point to Kazan) but for the most part, they don't. Gutman tells us that as a group they are "confused and exhausted," at cocktail time they "drift downstairs on the wings of gin and the lift . . . and exchange notes again on fashionable couturiers and custom tailors, restaurants, vintages of wine, hair-dressers, plastic surgeons, girls and young men susceptible to offers. . . ." The Romantics are aware of their impotence but make no attempt to change. Only Kilroy attempts to oppose the power of the state; otherwise, their acts of gallantry are meant solely for each other.

Williams's choice to remain allusive in his politics makes *Camino Real* very much a play of, "On the one hand—but on the other . . .". Don Quix-otes cries, "The time for retreat never comes!" while Marguerite Gautier, famous courtesan, believes that, "Bohemia has no banner. It survives by discretion." Of all the Romantics, only the Baron risks being seen talking to Kilroy, whose arrival on the Camino Real attracts the unwanted attention of the police. Jacques Casanova is outraged at the brutal treatment meted out to the Survivor, but as the man is murdered in the street, the famous libertine sits on the terrace of the Siete Mares hotel, watching. "My heart is too tired to break," he says, sipping his brandy. The Romantics want to live life honorably, but lack the bravery to face down Gutman and engage in what is now called "regime change."

Of the many poetic images in Williams's work, the flock of birds in flight is perhaps the most constant. The flying birds symbolize freedom of all sorts: to love, to think, to dream, to change, to *be*. In *Camino Real*, the birds aren't free, they're captive. Sancho Panza warns Don Quixote, "—there are no birds in the country except wild birds that are tamed and kept in—[. . .] *Cages!*" Marguerite, anxious to flee both the desperate at-mosphere of the Camino and her feelings for Jacques (commitment of any kind comes hard for most of the Romantics), tells him, "Caged birds accept each other but flight is what they long for." The Baron complains about the bourgeois guests at the Siete Mares, "who rap on the wall if canaries sing in your bed-springs after midnight." One of the play's high points is the appearance of Lord Byron, who, in Williams's hands, is a poet who has squandered his gifts on the sensual prizes with which life has rewarded (or trapped) him. He is striking out for unknown territory in the hope of rediscovering "the old pure music" that once gave his life and work mean-ing. Several porters carry his luggage, which consists, the stage direc-tion tells us, of "mainly caged birds." "*Make voyages!*" he cries. "*Attempt them!*—there's nothing else . . . " If the poet finds his voice again in new lands, finds the courage to speak the forbidden word, perhaps the birds will burst the bars of their cages as the violets break through the mountain rocks as the play ends.

The question is, can honor be found in acts of generosity between one person and another, such as the one Marguerite finally bestows on Jacques, and in the poet's quest for authenticity? Or is Byron's grand exit from the repressive and cruel Camino Real just . . . flight?

Williams wrote in *The New York Times* that *Camino Real* was, "noth-

ing more nor less than my conception of the time and world that I live in."
He told the *Saturday Review*, "each time I return [to the United States] I
sense a further reduction in human liberties, which I guess is reflected in
the revisions of the play. . . . It is, I guess you could say, a prayer for the wild
at heart kept in cages . . . The romantic should have the spirit of anarchy
and not let the world drag him down to its level."

The world that Williams wrote about is a world where people fear
the cost of speaking out on behalf of others. It's a world where empathy
is in short supply and few have the courage to say, "Hermano," while the
Gutmans of the world boast, in one way or another, "I have mine and the
hell with you." It's a world, in other words, like the one we live in now.
"*Make voyages! Attempt them!* —there's nothing else . . . " Lord Byron's
final words, as he and his caged birds head out of the Camino Real for
"Terra Incognita," are "THIS WAY!"

Which way? Private gestures of personal kindness, or public acts of
civic bravery? Which is more honorable, more necessary in times of trouble? Is it a matter of either/or? Or of both/and? Williams, wanting to be
allusive, doesn't say. Perhaps there's a clue in the fact that in that time and
place, he wrote the play and asked us the question.

MICHAEL PALLER
AMERICAN CONSERVATORY THEATER

A CHRONOLOGY

1907   June 3: Cornelius Coffin Williams and Edwina Estelle Dakin marry in Columbus, Mississippi.

1909   November 19: Sister, Rose Isabelle Williams, is born in Columbus, Mississippi.

1911   March 26: Thomas Lanier Williams III is born in Columbus, Mississippi.

1918   July: Williams family moves to St. Louis, Missouri.

1919   February 21: Brother, Walter Dakin Williams, is born in St. Louis, Missouri.

1928   Short story "The Vengeance of Nitocris" is published in *Weird Tales* magazine.

         July: Williams' grandfather, Walter Edwin Dakin (1857-1954), takes young Tom on a tour of Europe.

1929   September: Begins classes at the University of Missouri at Columbia.

1930   Writes the one-act play *Beauty is the Word* for a local contest.

1932   Summer: Fails ROTC and is taken out of college by his father and put to work as a clerk at the International Shoe Company.

1936   January: Enrolls in extension courses at Washington University, St. Louis.

1937   March 18 and 20: First full-length play, *Candles to the Sun*, is produced by the Mummers, a semi-professional theater company in St. Louis.

         September: Transfers to the University of Iowa.

         November 30 and December 4: *Fugitive Kind* is performed by the Mummers.

1938   Graduates from the University of Iowa with a degree in English.

Completes the play, *Not About Nightingales.*

1939   *Story* magazine publishes "The Field of Blue Children" with the first printed use of his professional name, "Tennessee Williams."

Receives an award from the Group Theatre for a group of short plays collectively titled *American Blues*, which leads to his association with Audrey Wood, his agent for the next thirty-two years.

1940   January through June: Studies playwriting with John Gassner at the New School for Social Research in New York City.

December 30: *Battle of Angels*, starring Miriam Hopkins, suffers a disastrous first night during its out-of-town tryout in Boston and closes shortly thereafter.

1942   December: At a cocktail party thrown by Lincoln Kirstein in New York, meets James Laughlin, founder of New Directions, who is to become Williams' lifelong friend and publisher.

1943   Drafts a screenplay, *The Gentleman Caller*, while under contract in Hollywood with Metro Goldwyn Mayer: rejected by the studio, he later rewrites it as *The Glass Menagerie.*

October 13: A collaboration with his friend Donald Windham, *You Touched Me!* (based on a story by D.H. Lawrence), premieres at the Cleveland Playhouse.

1944   December 26: *The Glass Menagerie* opens in Chicago starring Laurette Taylor.

A group of poems titled "The Summer Belvedere" is published in *Five Young American Poets, 1944.* (All books listed here are published by New Directions unless otherwise indicated.)

1945   March 25: *Stairs to the Roof* premieres at the Pasadena Playhouse in California.

March 31: *The Glass Menagerie* opens on Broadway and goes on to win the Drama Critics Circle Award for best play of the year.

September 25: *You Touched Me!* opens on Broadway, and is later published by Samuel French.

December: 27 Wagons Full of Cotton and Other Plays is published.

1947   Summer: Meets Frank Merlo (1929-1963) in Provincetown—starting in 1948 they become lovers and companions, and remain together for fourteen years.

December 3: *A Streetcar Named Desire,* directed by Elia Kazan and starring Jessica Tandy, Marlon Brando, Kim Hunter and Karl Malden, opens on Broadway to rave reviews and wins the Pulitzer Prize and the Drama Critics Circle Award.

1948   October 6: *Summer and Smoke* opens on Broadway and closes in just over three months.

1949   January: *One Arm and Other Stories* is published.

1950   The novel *The Roman Spring of Mrs. Stone* is published.

The film version of *The Glass Menagerie* is released.

1951   February 3: *The Rose Tattoo* opens on Broadway starring Maureen Stapleton and Eli Wallach and wins the Tony Award for best play of the year.

The film version of *A Streetcar Named Desire* is released starring Vivian Leigh as Blanche and Marlon Brando as Stanley.

1952   April 24: A revival of *Summer and Smoke* directed by Jose Quintero and starring Geraldine Page opens off-Broadway at the Circle at the Square and is a critical success.

        The National Institute of Arts and Letters inducts Williams as a member.

1953   March 19: *Camino Real* opens on Broadway and after a harsh critical reception closes within two months.

1954   A book of stories, *Hard Candy*, is published in August.

1955   March 24: *Cat on a Hot Tin Roof* opens on Broadway directed by Elia Kazan and starring Barbara Bel Geddes, Ben Gazzara and Burl Ives. *Cat* wins the Pulitzer Prize and the Drama Critics Circle Award.

        The film version of *The Rose Tattoo*, for which Anna Magnani later wins an Academy Award, is released.

1956   The film *Baby Doll*, with a screenplay by Williams and directed by Elia Kazan, is released amid some controversy and is blacklisted by Catholic leader Cardinal Spellman.

        June: *In the Winter of Cities*, Williams' first book of poetry, is published.

1957   March 21: *Orpheus Descending*, a revised version of *Battle of Angels*, directed by Harold Clurman, opens on Broadway but closes after two months.

1958   February 7: *Suddenly Last Summer* and *Something Unspoken* open off-Broadway under the collective title *Garden District*.

        The film version of *Cat on a Hot Tin Roof* is released.

1959   March 10: *Sweet Bird of Youth* opens on Broadway and runs for three months.

        The film version of *Suddenly Last Summer*, with a screenplay by Gore Vidal, is released.

1960   November 10: The comedy *Period of Adjustment* opens on Broadway and runs for over four months.

The film version of *Orpheus Descending* is released under the title *The Fugitive Kind*.

1961   December 29: *The Night of the Iguana* opens on Broadway and runs for nearly ten months.

The film versions of *Summer and Smoke* and *The Roman Spring of Mrs. Stone* are released.

1962   The film versions of *Sweet Bird of Youth* and *Period of Adjustment* are released.

1963   January 15: *The Milk Train Doesn't Stop Here Anymore* opens on Broadway and closes immediately due to a blizzard and a newspaper strike. It is revived January 1, 1964 in a Broadway production starring Tallulah Bankhead and Tab Hunter and closes within a week.

September: Frank Merlo dies of lung cancer.

1964   The film version of *Night of the Iguana* is released.

1966   February 22: *Slapstick Tragedy* (*The Mutilated* and *The Gnädiges Fräulein*) runs on Broadway for less than a week.

December: A novella and stories are published under the title *The Knightly Quest*.

1968   March 27: *Kingdom of Earth* opens on Broadway under the title *The Seven Descents of Myrtle*.

The film version of *The Milk Train Doesn't Stop Here Anymore* is released under the title *Boom!*

1969   May 11: *In the Bar of a Tokyo Hotel* opens off-Broadway and runs for three weeks.

Committed by his brother Dakin for three months to the Renard Psychiatric Division of Barnes Hospital in St. Louis.

The film version of *Kingdom of Earth* is released under the title *The Last of the Mobile Hot Shots.*

Awarded Doctor of Humanities degree by the University of Missouri and a Gold Medal for Drama by the American Academy of Arts and Letters.

1970   February: A book of plays, *Dragon Country*, is published.

1971   Williams breaks with his agent Audrey Wood. Bill Barnes assumes his representation, and then later Mitch Douglas.

1972   April 2: *Small Craft Warnings* opens off-Broadway.

Williams is given a Doctor of Humanities degree by the University of Hartford.

1973   March 1: *Out Cry*, the revised version of *The Two-Character Play*, opens on Broadway.

1974   September: *Eight Mortal Ladies Possessed*, a book of short stories, is published.

Williams is presented with an Entertainment Hall of Fame Award and a Medal of Honor for Literature from the National Arts Club.

1975   The novel *Moise and the World of Reason* is published by Simon and Schuster and Williams' *Memoirs* is published by Doubleday.

1976   January 20: *This Is (An Entertainment)* opens in San Francisco at the American Conservatory Theater.

June: *The Red Devil Battery Sign* closes during its out-of-town tryout in Boston.

November 23: *Eccentricities of a Nightingale*, a rewritten version of *Summer and Smoke*, opens in New York.

April: Williams' second volume of poetry, *Androgyne, Mon Amour*, is published.

1977   May 11: *Vieux Carrè* opens on Broadway and closes within two weeks.

1978   *Tiger Tail* premieres at the Alliance Theater in Atlanta, Georgia and a revised version premieres the following year at the Hippodrome Theater in Gainsville, Florida.

1979   January 10: *A Lovely Sunday for Creve Coeur* opens off-Broadway.

       Kirche, Küche, Kinder premieres off-Broadway at the Jean Cocteau Repertory Theater.

       Williams is presented with a Lifetime Achievement Award at the Kennedy Center Honors in Washington by President Jimmy Carter.

1980   January 25: *Will Mr. Merriwether Return from Memphis?* premieres for a limited run at the Tennessee Williams Performing Arts Center in Key West, Florida.

       March 26: Williams' last Broadway play, *Clothes for a Summer Hotel*, opens and closes after 15 performances.

1981   August 24: *Something Cloudy, Something Clear* premieres off-Broadway at the Jean Cocteau Repertory Theater.

1982   May 8: The second of two versions of *A House Not Meant to Stand* opens for a limited run at the Goodman Theater in Chicago.

1983   February 24: Williams is found dead in his room at the Hotel Elysee in New York City. It is determined from an autopsy that the playwright died from asphyxiation, choking on a plastic medicine cap. Williams is later buried in St. Louis.

1984   July: *Stopped Rocking and Other Screenplays* is published.

1985   November: *Collected Stories*, with an introduction by Gore Vidal, is published.

1995   The first half of Lyle Leverich's important biography, *Tom: The Unknown Tennessee Williams* is published by Crown Publishers.

1996   September 5: Rose Isabelle Williams dies in Tarrytown, New York.

   September 5: *The Notebook of Trigorin*, in a version revised by Williams, opens at the Cincinnati Playhouse in the Park.

1998   March 5: *Not About Nightingales* premieres at the Royal National Theatre in London, directed by Trevor Nunn, later moves to Houston, Texas, and opens November 25, 1999 on Broadway.

1999   November: *Spring Storm* is published.

2000   May: *Stairs to the Roof* is published.

   November: *The Selected Letters of Tennessee Williams, Volume I* is published.

2001   June: *Fugitive Kind* is published.

2002   April: *Collected Poems* is published.

2004   August: *Candles to the Sun* is published.

   November: *The Selected Letters of Tennessee Williams, Volume II* is published.

2005   April: *Mister Paradise and Other One-Act Plays* is published.

2008   April: *A House Not Meant to Stand* and *The Traveling Companion and Other Plays* are published.

   May 20: Walter Dakin Williams dies at the age of 89 in Belleville, Illinois.